FIRSTBORN

FIRSTBORN

TOR SEIDLER

A CAITLYN DLOUHY BOOK

ATHENEUM BOOKS FOR YOUNG READERS

New York   London   Toronto   Sydney   New Delhi

IN REMEMBRANCE OF
JEAN CRAIGHEAD GEORGE

ATHENEUM BOOKS FOR YOUNG READERS • An imprint of Simon & Schuster Children's Publishing Division • 1230 Avenue of the Americas, New York, New York 10020 • This book is a work of fiction. Any references to historical events, real people, or real places are used fictitiously. Other names, characters, places, and events are products of the author's imagination, and any resemblance to actual events or places or persons, living or dead, is entirely coincidental. • Text copyright © 2015 by Tor Seidler • Illustrations copyright © 2015 by Chris Sheban • Map illustration copyright © 2015 by Drew Willis • All rights reserved, including the right of reproduction in whole or in part in any form. • ATHENEUM BOOKS FOR YOUNG READERS is a registered trademark of Simon & Schuster, Inc. • Atheneum logo is a trademark of Simon & Schuster, Inc. • For information about special discounts for bulk purchases, please contact Simon & Schuster Special Sales at 1-866-506-1949 or business@simonandschuster.com. • The Simon & Schuster Speakers Bureau can bring authors to your live event. For more information or to book an event, contact the Simon & Schuster Speakers Bureau at 1-866-248-3049 or visit our website at www.simonspeakers.com. • Also available in an Atheneum Books for Young Readers hardcover edition. • Book design by Debra Sfetsios-Conover • The text for this book is set in Adobe Garamond Pro. • The illustrations for this book are rendered in graphite and pastel. • Manufactured in the United States of America • 0116 MTN • First Atheneum Books for Young Readers paperback edition March 2016 • 10 9 8 7 6 5 4 3 2 1 • The Library of Congress has cataloged the hardcover edition as follows: Seidler, Tor. • Firstborn / Tor Seidler ; illustrated by Chris Sheban. — First edition. • pages cm • Summary: "A wolf pack's alpha male gets a disappointing surprise when his first born son is not like a normal wolf, but rather one who has fallen for a coyote."— Provided by publisher. • [1. Wolves—Fiction. 2. Montana—Fiction.] I. Sheban, Chris, illustrator. II. Title. • PZ7.S45526Fi 2015 • [Fic]—dc23 • 2014009659 • ISBN 978-1-4814-1017-5 (hc) • ISBN 978-1-4814-1018-2 (pbk) • ISBN 978-1-4814-1019-9 (eBook)

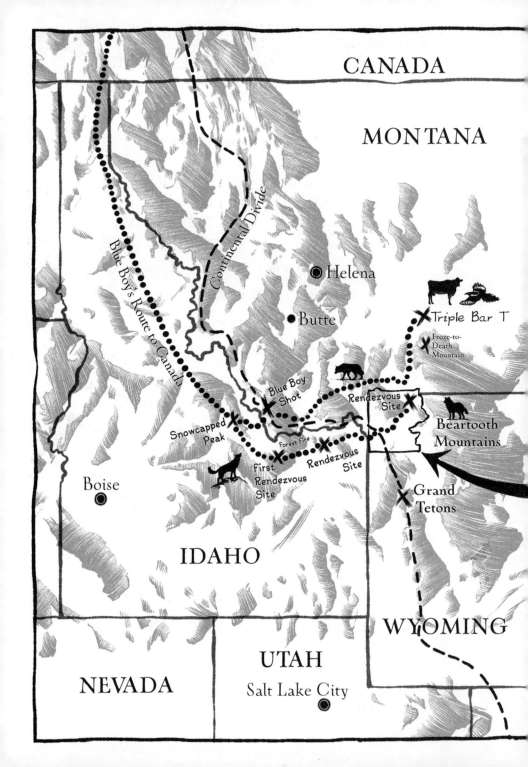

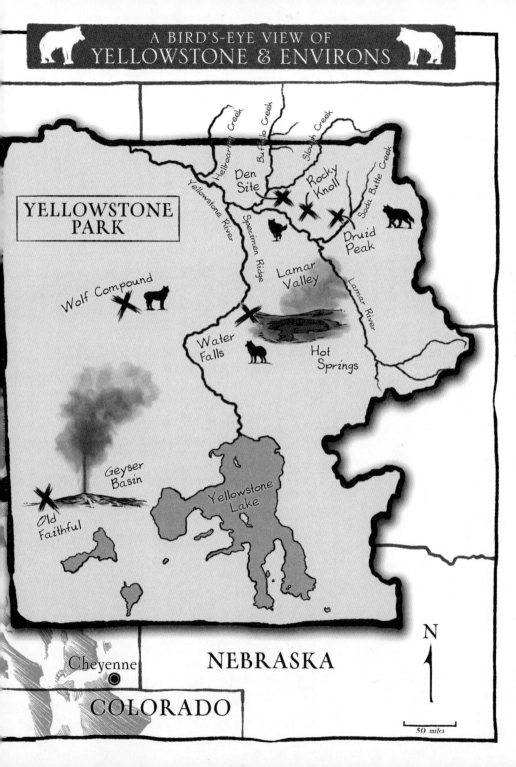

1

"COME SEE, MAX!" MY MOTHER CRIED. "Max, come see!"

My father landed on the rim of the nest and held something over me in his black beak. I'd just broken through my shell. There were several other grayish-green shells around me, all still intact. I craned my neck, grabbed the morsel out of my father's beak, and gulped it down.

"Isn't she the most adorable little magpie in the whole world?" my mother crooned. "Cute, cute, cute! What shall we call her?"

"Up to you, Mag," said my father. "You did most of the work."

"How about Maggie?"

"Perfect."

I gawped at them in disbelief. Here I was, a minute-old magpie, with a mother named Mag and a father named Max, and they were calling me Maggie! My only consolation was that they weren't much more imaginative with my five siblings. As my brothers and sisters hatched around me, they were dubbed Mark, Marge, Mandy, Mack, and Matt.

On a brighter note, I wasn't just first out of the egg—I was also the first of the brood to make it to the edge of the nest.

"What's this place called?" I asked, looking out.

"Home," my mother said. "Isn't it glorious, glorious, glorious?"

It was quite a view, though of course I had little to compare it to.

"What are those green things?" I said, peering straight down.

"Branches. We're in a pine tree."

She pointed out other pine trees, a farmhouse, a smaller structure called a henhouse, a bigger one called a barn, and two tall things with egg-shaped tops called silos. Between the silos was a glittering ribbon of blue. In the distance there were fenced-in fields, some trees with leaves instead of needles, and vast expanses of open range.

"What are the four-legged beasts?" I asked.

"Cattle."

"Where's their nest?"

"There," she said, pointing her beak at the barn.

The small boxlike thing on top of the barn was called a cupola, and the thing on top of that was a weather vane. The weather vane had a bird perched on it.

"Is that a magpie?" I asked.

"That homely old thing? He's a crow."

Hopping onto the sunny side of the nest, my mother spread her wings and flicked her tail.

"You're the most beautiful ma in the world," cooed my brother Matt.

How many mothers did he know, I wondered—though, in fact, ours was pretty striking. Her black-and-white plumage had a hint of iridescent green, and her tail was long and graceful.

She and my father devoted the next few days to bringing us lovely insects and succulent bits of carrion. As our fluff turned to feathers, our parents warned us of creatures to avoid once we left the nest. "Keep a sharp eye out for eagles and foxes." "Watch out for hawks and coyotes."

"Foxes and housecats." "Coyotes and rattlesnakes and eagles." "Did we mention foxes?"

As we grew, the nest got more and more cramped, and despite the looming perils, I yearned to be free of it. But the only way out of the nest was by air, and my first attempt at flying was a disaster. If not for a well-placed bough, I'd have broken my neck. I did better on my second try, however, and by the time I was a month old, I was giving my siblings flying lessons.

Life without wings must be a bitter thing. You'd miss out on not only the freedom, but the perspective. Flying lets you see from close up or far away. You can zoom up to things and, if you don't like the look of them, zoom away. At first I steered well clear of cattle. They're enormous, and smelly. But one day I saw my father alight on one. I fluttered down and landed gingerly beside him.

"They're so dull, they don't mind," he said. "Dig in, Maggie."

The beast was covered with ticks. It was a feast.

Horses and dogs pick up ticks as well, but horses are less docile than cattle, with dangerous tails, and dogs are absolute monsters, to be avoided at all cost. Though humans pick up fewer ticks, I developed a soft spot for them anyway. The silly creatures were always discarding tasty garbage.

By summer my whole clutch had left the nest for good. Sadly, the creek that wound between the silos dried up, so we had to drink from the cattle trough. Blech! And except for a few trees, the whole landscape turned dull brown, with dust devils swirling across it. Then came winter, and everything turned stark white. The days were short and cold, the nights long and even colder.

The cattle huddled in the barn. One day I noticed steam leaking out of the cupola. The homely old crow was still on the weather vane, and he was more than twice my size, but crows hadn't been on my parents' list of creatures to avoid, and I couldn't see why he should hog all the heat. Besides, I'd become as handsome as my mother, and I figured he might be flattered by a visit from someone so much better-looking.

I flew over and landed on the cupola. The steam felt wonderful, even if it stank, but the crow glared down from the weather vane.

"Scram," he said.

"Why?" I said. "There's plenty of room."

"I can't abide magpies."

"What's wrong with magpies?"

"They're empty-headed chatterboxes."

"Who says?"

"Ask anybody."

I flew off and found a starling perched on the ice-glazed swing set behind the farmhouse.

"What sort of reputation do magpies have?" I asked.

"Thieving hoarders," the starling said.

This wasn't very flattering, but at least it didn't confirm the crow. I flew over to a thrush poking around by the garbage cans behind the house and asked her the same question.

"Empty-headed chatterboxes," she said.

I gulped.

A buzzard on a telephone pole gave me the same answer. I returned to my favorite ponderosa pine to nurse my bruised ego. At sunset I tucked my head under my wing as usual, but I couldn't sleep. Thinking back, I realized my parents and siblings did chatter a lot. I remembered my mother calling home "glorious, glorious, glorious." Now that I'd experienced a sweltering, dull-brown summer and a snowy, sub-zero winter, I had to question that. But even if some magpies didn't think before they spoke, did that mean *I* was like that?

In the morning I flew to the cupola, determined to prove the crow wrong, but he wasn't on the weather vane. While I was basking in the smelly warmth, I spotted him down below, walking out from between two bulging roots of an old cottonwood tree. I figured he must have a food cache there. Out on the sunstruck snow he opened his impressive wings and pushed off.

The lower part of the weather vane was four arrows pointing in different directions. The top part was shaped like a horse. The horse moved in the wind and squeaked when the crow landed on it.

"Scat," the crow said.

I ignored him. He ruffed up his feathers, doubling his size. I crouched, ready to take off. Down below, a door banged. A human came out of the farmhouse, followed by a dog. They got into one of their vehicles. It rumbled to life, spewing a bluish cloud into the clear air, and rolled away, the tires kicking up the dry snow just as they kicked up the dust in the summer. At the end of a long straightaway the vehicle passed through a gate and turned left.

By the time the vehicle was out of sight, the crow had deflated to his normal size. I stayed put for about an hour, till I was nice and toasty, before flying away.

When I returned to the cupola the next morning, the crow was gone again. Like the day before, he soon emerged from his food cache under the cottonwood and flapped up to the weather vane. He gave me a sour look but didn't ruff up his feathers. I warmed myself for an hour or so, keeping my beak resolutely shut.

This went on for a week. I never said a word on the cupola—till one day a sharp cracking sound startled me into blurting out, "What was that?"

"A rifle," the crow said.

Not wanting to sound empty-headed, I didn't ask what this was. Before long a human wearing a cap with earflaps came hustling around the side of the barn. Earflaps lifted a long, glinting thing to his shoulder, and another crack rang out.

"Missed again," the crow said, chuckling.

A flash of red crossed one of the snowy fields.

"There was a fox in the henhouse," the crow said.

So that was a fox, I thought, remembering my parents' warnings.

The next morning I had to wait out a blizzard, and by the time I arrived at the cupola, the crow was on his weather vane. He didn't look particularly annoyed, so I asked him his name.

"Jackson," he grunted. "You?"

"Maggie."

"Maggie the magpie?"

"I know," I said with a sigh.

The next day was too windy to do anything but huddle on the lee side of my ponderosa pine. But the wind died down overnight, and the following day I rejoined the crow atop the barn.

"Quite a blow," he commented.

Though the temperature was well below zero, I sensed him thawing toward me. "How long have you lived at home, Jackson?" I asked.

"At home?"

"Here. This place."

"You mean the Triple Bar T?"

"The Triple Bar T?"

"You never checked the gate?"

I did now, flying straight out the long driveway. Over the gate was a sign emblazoned with: ≡ T.

The next day I asked him what the weather vane was for, and he used it to teach me north from south and east from west. To the south there were large bumps on the horizon. These were called the Beartooth Mountains. Beyond them was a place called Wyoming. I asked if Wyoming was as big as the Triple Bar T.

"Bigger," Jackson said. "The Triple Bar T's just a ranch. Wyoming's a state. We're in the state of Montana."

"Is Montana bigger than Wyoming?"

"Yes."

"What's that way?" I asked, pointing my beak to the west.

"Idaho."

"Is Montana bigger?"

"Yes."

"And that way?" I said, pointing north.

"Canada."

"Montana's bigger?"

"No. But Canada's not a state, it's a country."

The discomfiting truth was sinking in: I *was* empty-headed.

The cupola became my school. I learned a lot about geography—and other things too. One day, for example, I asked Jackson why cattle were so dull, and he explained that they have no souls.

"How come?"

"Only winged creatures have souls."

This made perfect sense. "What about chickens?" I said. "They have wings, but they can barely fly."

"A question I grappled with, myself," he said, giving me an almost appreciative look. "After conversing with a few, I concluded they don't."

"How do you know so much, Jackson?"

"I don't. At least compared to my friend."

I was surprised to hear he had one. Most crows are sociable and hang out in gangs, but Jackson seemed very solitary. I'd heard other crows cawing to him, but he never answered.

"Who's your friend?" I said.

"Miranda," he said.

Miranda! If only my parents had had a little imagination, I could have had a beautiful name like that. "She's a crow?" I said.

"A parrot."

"What's a parrot?"

"A tropical bird—stunningly beautiful. Humans keep them in cages. But hers was by the window, and in the summertime, when the window was open, we talked up a storm. I picked up a lot, especially about humans. She even taught me their language."

This was astounding. Their language was very tricky. "She's not in a cage anymore?"

"She's free now."

"But you still see her?"

"We talk every day."

Though I couldn't help being jealous of the parrot's name and abilities, I hoped to meet her, but I sensed Jackson might be stingy with her company. I decided to keep my eye out for places he went other than the weather vane and the food cache. If Miranda was a tropical bird, she might well live in the barn, out of the cold. But in the winter the barn was shut up tight.

Eventually the snow began to melt. One day the doors to the hayloft swung open. But when I flew in, all I saw were a couple of bats, a gang of swallows, and hundreds of smelly steers.

The cattle soon came out to graze in the fields. Chicks started bumbling around on the coop's chicken-wired porch. Humans started doing all sorts of noisy things around the place. They shouted at one another a lot, and thanks to Jackson's coaching, I began to decipher some of their words. As spring progressed, they set up a big scale to weigh livestock for the market. They shouted out the weights, and little by little I deciphered the differences. By summer I was a whiz at numbers.

Even noisier than their shouting was their target practice. Earflaps set up a target and showed a smaller human in a red cap how to fire the rifle at it. The silhouette on the target was a lot bigger than a fox, more like a large dog.

"I thought humans were fond of those fiends," I said.

"I believe it's a wolf," Jackson said. "Miranda told me they're worried about them."

"What's a wolf?"

"They're like dogs, only wilder and more ferocious. They kill cattle and sheep. The ranchers hate them."

"Do they kill birds?"

"If they could catch us, they probably would."

"Do they live around here?" I asked uneasily.

"The ranchers wiped them out a long time ago."

"Then why are they worried?"

"Because of Yellowstone," Jackson said.

Yellowstone, I learned next, was a national park just south of the Beartooth Mountains, mostly in Wyoming. Certain humans wanted to reintroduce wolves there— to restore the "balance of nature," whatever that meant. The ranchers were dead set against it, but according to Miranda, the wolf lovers had prevailed, and now the ranchers were afraid the reintroduced wolves might venture out of the park and attack their livestock.

But I had more pressing concerns than creatures I'd never laid eyes on. Of my brood, four of us had made it through our first winter. A hawk had picked off Mack last summer, and not long afterward Mark had ended up flattened against the radiator of one of the humans' vehicles. But now, as the leaves unfurled on the cotton-wood tree, Matt and Mandy each paired off, and the two new couples started building nests of their own. Though I liked to think of myself as different from my siblings, I'd always been first at everything and disliked suddenly slipping behind. A handsome young magpie named Dan kept pestering me, saying how pretty my tail feathers were. I gave in.

The nest Dan built in my favorite ponderosa pine had a waterproof hood of interwoven twigs. It put my parents' nest to shame. But he no sooner finished it than he started filling it with useless odds and ends collected from around the ranch: wadded-up gum wrappers, screws, washers, pennies, bottle caps. When I asked what the trash was for, he said, "It's pretty!" This totally undermined his compliments on my tail feathers. I got the queasy feeling that he fit the "thieving hoarder" profile. Every time I chucked something out, he retrieved it, so when the eggs came there was barely room for them.

Dan refused to do any egg sitting. I was stuck in the nest night and day with all his bric-a-brac. He did bring me food, but my ordeal went on for weeks. With the melting snow the lovely ribbon of blue reappeared, but I couldn't even go down for a drink. Interesting bird species whizzed by, but I couldn't find out if they were flying up from the south or down from Canada. Meanwhile I had to watch my single sister, Marge, doing loop-di-loops between the silos. Worst of all, I didn't get to chat with Jackson.

I was looking forward to naming the baby girls—Dan had dibs on naming the boys—but when the eggs hatched there was only one girl. Dan named the boys Danny, Denny, Dash, Del, and Dave. I named the girl Anastasia. I was run ragged foraging for the six of them. And then I had to help teach them to fly. What a relief when they finally left the nest for good!

"We did a pretty good job, don't you think?" I said.

"Want to double down?" said Dan.

"Double down?"

"Get started on another clutch."

"Another clutch!" I cried. "Are you crazy?"

"Lots of magpies do two clutches a year," he said with a defensive flick of his tail. "But if you insist we can wait till next spring."

His assumption that we'd still be together in the spring shouldn't have surprised me. A lot of magpies mate for life. My parents had always been inseparable. But the thought of spending my whole life with Dan and his junk made me shudder.

The next day I flew over to the cupola.

"Been a while," Jackson said.

"Hatchlings," I explained.

"How are they?"

"Gone, thank goodness. How are you?"

"Fine."

"Um, I was wondering . . . have you always been single?"

"Depends how you define single. Why do you ask?"

"Well, Dan was talking about having more kids next spring—and it's sent me into a tailspin. Is something the matter with me?"

"For most magpies that would be a bit odd. But, of course, if you were an ordinary magpie, I wouldn't be talking to you."

This cheered me up some.

"The thing is, it's hard to be different and the same at once," he said, reading my mind. "You generally have to opt for one."

I suppose I'd wanted to be both. But trying to be like my siblings had just made me miserable. "Would it be disloyal of me not to stick with Dan?" I said.

"Well, if I've learned anything over the years, it's this: you can't be loyal to others if you're not loyal to your own nature first."

I was touched by his sharing his wisdom with me. I almost felt like hopping up and giving him a peck on the cheek, but of course he would have been appalled by a display like that, so I decided to get him something nice to eat instead. I flew over to the cattle pen and settled on one of the steers.

As I was storing ticks in the pouch under my tongue, a flash of brilliant blue fell from the sky and landed on a nearby wire fence. The fence was electric, but I swear the current hopped over and shivered through me.

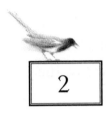

2

IT WAS A BRIGHT SPRING DAY, but the blue sky was lackluster compared to the bird on the fence. He was the most gorgeous thing I'd ever seen. However, the electricity may have bothered him, for he soon took wing and headed out over the open range. I sat on the steer gawking after him till he disappeared.

When I got back to the cupola, Jackson accepted the ticks politely, but I could tell he wasn't thrilled with them.

"I just saw the most amazing bird," I said.

"Mountain bluebird?" Jackson guessed. "I saw him this morning. He likes the flies and gnats the cattle attract."

I didn't see the mountain bluebird again that day,

but the next morning I spotted him on the farmhouse chimney. I wanted to fly over and introduce myself but knew I wouldn't be able to utter a sound. He was just that dazzling.

I couldn't eat the rest of the day. That night I barely slept.

"You don't look so hot," Dan said in the morning.

It was as if I had a sickness. But I couldn't very well discuss it with him, so I flew over to the cupola and waited for Jackson. While he was off visiting his food cache or the mysterious Miranda, the skies opened. I took shelter in the hayloft. A minute later the bluebird shot in out of the rain and landed a few feet away.

"A real snorter," he said, shaking droplets off his gorgeous plumage.

I swallowed. "Do you . . ."

"Do I?"

"Do you l-like it around here?" I stammered. "I mean, when it's not pouring."

He plucked a bug from the loose hay and gobbled it down. "It's not bad," he said.

I was dying to know his name. But if I asked, he would ask mine.

"Been around here long?" he said.

"All my life."

"Ah. Then you wouldn't have seen the ocean."

"What's that?"

"They say it's the biggest thing on earth. Very blue."

"As blue as you?" I said, wide-eyed.

"I haven't seen it yet."

"It sounds worth a visit."

"I'm glad you think so."

My heart raced at the thought that he might like me to see it with him. "Which way is it?" I asked.

He pointed his beak out of the hayloft, which faced west.

"Have you traveled a lot?" I asked.

"A fair amount," he said.

He'd flown above the tree line, tasted a salty lake, and seen a city that was bright as noon at midnight. While he was relating his adventures, the rain let up.

"Well, I better get going," he said, shaking a fleck of straw off his right wing. "What's your name, anyway?"

"Maggie," I mumbled.

"Maggie the magpie."

"It wasn't my choice. How about you?"

"Trilby."

Trilby! After he'd gone, all I could think about was

using this radiant new word. That night I practiced saying it under my breath: "Morning, Trilby." "Hi, Trilby." "What's up, Trilby?" But the next day I never got to use it. He was nowhere to be found. When I didn't see him again the following morning, I was frantic. Once Jackson landed on his weather vane, I flew straight to the cupola.

"I don't suppose you've seen that bluebird?" I said, trying to sound nonchalant.

"The barn swallows chased him away yesterday," Jackson said. "Didn't like him horning in on their bugs."

I gasped. Jackson gave me a look before pointing his beak to the west. "He went that way."

I didn't go chasing after Trilby right away. First I swooped down onto the hay bailer and pretended to peck seeds on the conveyor belt. But after a decent interval had passed, I flew off to the west.

The closest I'd ever come to leaving the ranch was when I'd gone to read the sign over the gate, so my heart fluttered when I flew over a split-rail fence marking the end of the property. I passed over a deep, wooded ravine, and then I was out on the open range.

I was used to flying in brief bursts. It was quite a strain to flap along for hours on end, stopping only now and then for a quick bite. But I saw wonders: a railroad train hundreds of cars long; sheep ranches; windmills with perilous blades as long as silos; interstate highways; dammed-up lakes; endless wheat fields waving their golden tassels; towering grain elevators; great rivers with herons and osprey and even occasional human beings fishing in them.

At nightfall I found a ponderosa pine to rest my weary wings. You'd have thought my head would have been full of all the novelties I'd seen, but there only seemed to be room there for Trilby. The tree's familiar vanilla smell helped lull me to sleep, but Trilby quickly appeared in my dreams.

The next day I did more zigging and zagging. Meadowlarks gave me conflicting reports about bluebird sightings. It was dusk before I got a solid lead—from a tanager. She was sure she'd seen a bluebird heading for Butte.

"What's Butte?" I asked.

"A hive of humans. Just follow the highway."

I turned in for the night on a wooden brace behind a roadside billboard. In the morning I followed the tanager's advice, flying along above the westbound vehicles. At mid-day my heart leaped at the sight of Trilby perched alone on a telephone wire.

"Tri-i-i-ilby!" I cried, swooping down beside him.

"Maggie?" he said, looking put out. "What on earth are you doing here?"

My heart fell like a dropping. "I . . . I was thinking I might go with you to see the ocean."

He gave his azure shoulders a shrug. "Well, why not? Though I warn you, we'll get some strange looks—a bluebird and a magpie flying together. And it could be a very long way."

I'm not sure how much time went by before he said, "Better get going." When he took off, I didn't budge. He circled overhead a couple of times, then headed west. I couldn't even rotate my head to watch him fly away. It was as if I'd turned to stone.

I didn't leave that telephone wire all night. The highway down below wasn't busy, but every now and then headlights would light up the darkness and an eighteen-wheeler would storm by, ruffling my feathers. When the sun rose, I saw that the pale smudges to the west were snowcapped peaks, not clouds. I tortured myself with images of Trilby flying over them, achingly blue against the snow. My belly was empty, but I was too depressed to search for food. I sat there baking in the sun.

At dusk a herd of black-tailed deer wandered across the road. I knew they must carry ticks, but I didn't have the heart to fly down and check. By nightfall I was delirious, and my feet were cramped from gripping the wire so long. As I was about to pass out, a loud thunk startled me into alertness.

A deer was lying on the shoulder of the road right underneath me: a young doe. The vehicle that had hit her pulled off a little farther down the road, and a human got out of it and inspected the front of his vehicle. But he drove off without coming back to inspect the doe. She wasn't so much as twitching. The next headlights that passed by showed up a sheen of blood on her flank.

As the darkness thickened, the smell of the deer became so overpowering that I finally let go of the wire and dropped down onto the carcass. I took a nibble. Never in my life had I sampled anything so delicious. It was better than the tastiest garbage on the ranch.

I couldn't stop eating, and the feast restored me in spite of myself. The thought of Trilby's indifference was still like a cold claw around my heart, but its grip wasn't quite so paralyzing. I had an urge to tell someone what had happened, to get a little comforting. I could hardly expect Dan to sympathize, so I naturally thought of Jackson.

I spent the next day winging back to the east. That night I slept in a willow tree by a nearly dried-up pond. I got an early start the next morning and spotted the twin silos of the Triple Bar T shortly before midday. Jackson wasn't on the weather vane, so I automatically made for my ponderosa pine. Dan had collected more gimcracks since I'd left, so I could barely fit in the nest. He soon showed up with a paper clip.

"We thought you were dead!" he exclaimed, tossing in his latest find. "Where were you?"

"I took a little trip."

"A trip?"

"It turns out there's a lot to see outside the ranch."

"You went off sightseeing for days on end without even telling me?"

He flew off in a huff before I could think of an answer. Not that I had one. Now that I thought about it, I supposed I had been pretty inconsiderate. But the truth was, even though we'd had a clutch of eggs together, Dan didn't mean that much to me. And I knew I didn't mean nearly as much to him as his knickknacks.

I felt differently about Jackson. But in my absence he must have taken to spending more time with Miranda, for he didn't appear on his weather vane all afternoon. I did some reconnaissance. When I crossed paths with Dan— he had a shiny wing nut in his beak—he gave me the cold shoulder. He must have said something to the kids, for I got the same treatment from them. Who could blame them?

I spent that night in the hayloft, falling asleep to the painfully sweet memory of my brief interlude there with Trilby. In the morning I flew up to the cupola, hoping Jackson would come if he saw me. By noon he still hadn't, so I did something I'd never done before: I flew down to his food cache at the base of the cottonwood tree.

I ventured warily into a cavity between two of the tree's roots. As my eyes adjusted to the dimness, I saw no sign of Jackson other than a few dark covert feathers lining a bed of matted leaves. There was no food, either. Turning to go, I saw a cross stuck in the earth not far from the tree. Carved at the intersection of the two slats of wood was a crude *M*.

So this was why I'd never run across Miranda. Jackson came down here not to eat but to visit her grave.

I flew back up to the cupola and did something else I'd never done before: I called out his name, loud and clear. A squirrel scampering across the barn roof stopped and looked at me.

"That old crow?" he said.

"Yeah."

"He got shot a couple of days ago."

"Excuse me?"

"The smaller human in the red cap was taking pot-shots at him on the weather vane. Wonder of wonders, he hit him." The squirrel pointed his bushy tail to the north. "Afraid the bugs are getting at him."

Somehow I managed to open my wings and glide down over the eaves of the barn. A dark shape lay on the shady ground between a propane tank and a pile of old tires. I landed beside it and hissed:

"Off him!"

The insects ignored me. Most of them were crowded around a wound on Jackson's neck. I plucked the parasites off one by one. Normally I would have eaten them, but since they'd been nibbling on Jackson it seemed disrespectful, so I just spat them away.

Once Jackson was free of vermin, I looked into his right eye. It was cloudy, missing its old gleam. I wondered what his last thought had been.

I grabbed one of his scaly legs in my beak and dragged him a few inches along the ground. I rested. I grabbed the leg again and dragged him a few more inches.

It took a long time, but I finally got him to the corner of the barn. By then we were both pretty dusty. His murderer, Red Cap, was under the cottonwood tree, kicking a ball back and forth with his sister. As the sun lowered in the sky, another human called out that it was dinnertime. The boy and girl just kept kicking the ball. But when the call came again, shriller this time, they abandoned their play and went into the house.

By the time I got Jackson to his hideaway between the cottonwood's roots, the sun was near setting. I arranged him on the leafy bed with his head propped up, facing Miranda's cross, and then I sank down beside him. Now that I'd accomplished my mission, a tide of sorrow gushed over me. Jackson was gone, along with all his wonderful knowledge. And for what? A moment's satisfaction for a wanton boy—a soulless, earthbound creature! It was too cruel and stupid to think of, but I couldn't help myself.

As I stared out at the darkening sky, I began to feel sorry for myself. First my beautiful Trilby had rejected me, and now I'd lost my only friend in the world. I couldn't think what I had to live for and wished I could die along with the daylight.

Fate seemed to hear my thought.

A pair of close-set eyes glinted just outside the hideaway. They belonged to a fox. I was trapped. The only way out was past him. He knew it too. His snout twitched, and something like a grin played across his thin lips. As he let out a low snarl, baring razorlike teeth, I shook all over and tried to hide under Jackson.

With my head wedged between the crow's under feathers and some moldering leaves I heard a strangled yelp. I yanked my head out. The fox was gone. I flew out of there like a shot. Trotting off into the sunset with the fox in his mouth was a silhouette—just like the one on the humans' target.

3

I LANDED ON JACKSON'S WEATHER VANE with a hammering heart. One second I'd been a goner, fox food, and now here I was, sitting on top of the barn. I took long, slow sips of the still evening air. The western sky was the color of a ripe peach. In the east a nearly full moon was on the rise. The vast space in between was a deep, mysterious blue. Even if there wasn't a bird in the world who cared if I was alive or dead, I was glad to be alive.

Hardly a leaf was stirring on the cottonwood, but the hens were stirring in the henhouse, which was odd at this hour. Soon the cattle were lowing noisily in the pen with the electric fence, and horses whinnied in the paddock. A screen door banged. Earflaps came striding out across the yard. I didn't realize he had a rifle till the crack rang out. The cattle and hens and horses went crazy. The screen door banged again, and out bolted Red Cap and his sister. Earflaps's rifle erupted again. It went off four or five times before the humans trooped back toward the house.

"You really think it was a wolf, Dad?" asked Red Cap.

"Had to be," said Earflaps.

"Think you got him?"

"We'll have a look-see in the morning. If we didn't, we'll put the word out."

The humans went back inside. Soon the livestock settled down. Did that mean the wolf was dead? I hoped not, since I hadn't even had a chance to thank him for saving my life. But after the double traumas of Jackson's death and—nearly—my own, I was too exhausted to go searching, barely having the energy to flutter down to the hayloft for the night.

I woke when the cock crowed. The sky had flip-flopped. Now the moon was way over in the west, and the eastern horizon had a peachy glow. I went off to look for the wolf, dead or alive. As I wheeled around the ranch in widening circles, I passed over a steer skeleton, but no wolf carcass. My circling expanded beyond the ranch. The landscape was pretty baked out, but about a mile north of the Triple Bar T's gate I spotted the wolf sleeping on a swath of green in a creek bed. There wasn't much left of the creek at this time of the year. There wasn't much left of the fox either. I landed in an elderberry bush near its remains.

Though this was the first wolf I'd ever gotten a good look at, I could just tell he was a big one. As the sky brightened, I noticed he had a collar around his neck, like the dogs on the ranch, though the wolf's was thicker, with a lump on it. And I noticed that his glossy gray coat had a blue tinge to it.

His legs twitched, and then his eyes flickered open. They had a yellow gleam. When he stood up and shook himself, I almost felt sorry for the fox. This wolf, with his massive hindquarters, his sinewy neck and shoulders, and his long, powerful jaw, was clearly built for killing. He gave the fox remnants a disdainful sniff and took a slurp from the creek. As he started to trot away, I called after him:

"Hey. Thank you."

He looked back over his shoulder. The menacing glint in his eyes had me crouching in takeoff position.

"For what?" he growled.

I pointed my beak at the fox. "He was about to kill me when you grabbed him."

"You're welcome to him," the wolf said, and turned and trotted off to the north.

In fact, I was famished, and once the wolf was out of sight, I flew down and sampled the fox. He wasn't quite as good as the doe, but the meat was still fresh, and there was a certain satisfaction in eating someone who'd almost eaten me.

I was just finishing my breakfast when I heard rifle shots. The wolf came bounding back down the creek bed. I darted to the top of the elderberry bush. The wolf stopped nearby and crouched, the muscles tense on his back.

"The rancher at the Triple Bar T spread the word about you," I said, glad to see he hadn't been wounded.

He looked up suspiciously. I asked where he'd come from, and he pointed his snout to the south.

"I think you're supposed to stay there," I said, figuring he meant Yellowstone Park. "The ranchers up here don't like wolves."

Ignoring my advice, he set out to the north again, keeping lower to the ground this time. I stayed put. In a few minutes there were more rifle shots, and the wolf came running back down the creek bed.

"They're out for your hide," I told him. "Go back to Yellowstone. I don't think they'll shoot you there."

"I have to get home," he said.

"Where's that?"

He pointed his snout to the north.

"Canada?" I said. "Then how'd you get to Yellowstone?"

"I don't know," he said. "One minute I was hunting with my brother. The next, we're locked in a pen."

"Where's your brother?"

"Don't talk to me about that miserable cur."

"Well, what's so great about Canada?"

"I have five pups to feed."

"In that case, your best bet would probably be to go back to the Beartooth Mountains," I said, pointing south. "You could follow them to the west. There's another range over that way, in Idaho. I saw it with my own eyes. You might be able to follow those mountains into Canada."

He looked doubtful and headed off to the north again. Another volley of rifle shots brought him racing back. But he was nothing if not stubborn. He kept going back again and again all morning, till finally an all-terrain-vehicle with a pair of hunters in it came bouncing along in his wake. When the shooting started, I lit out of the creek bed, afraid the humans, who didn't seem very accurate with their bullets, would hit me by mistake.

As I neared the gate to the Triple Bar T, I heard

something and glanced back to see the wolf sprinting after me. A ways behind him was a dust cloud: the ATV, no doubt. Since I owed the wolf my life, the least I could do was try to help him, so I squawked and veered west. He followed. I led him to the ravine I'd flown over when I'd gone after Trilby.

The ravine was too rugged and thickly wooded for the humans' vehicle, but the wolf had no trouble negotiating the rocks and trees. He worked his way south. When he came to the end of the ravine, I warned him that there were ranches between there and the foothills of the Beartooth Mountains.

"Catch a nap," I suggested, "and head out after dark."

"I'm hungry," he said. "But thanks for the help."

He sloped off into the ravine, and I headed back to the Triple Bar T. Only when the barn and silos came into view did it occur to me that there was nothing for me there. Jackson was gone, and I'd alienated Dan and the kids. Perched on the split-rail fence, I stared bleakly at the weather vane, remembering what Jackson had said about being loyal to your own nature. I had a foreboding that it was my nature to go through life without a family, alone in the world.

✳ ✳ ✳

A few minutes later a guttural, blood-chilling cry at my back awakened another foreboding. The wolf must have ventured out of the ravine, must be in his death throes—though I hadn't heard any more rifle shots. I flew back to check and spotted the wolf on the east side of the ravine.

He wasn't dying. In fact, he was moving at a speed that impressed even me. He didn't make a sound as he zigzagged through the scrub pines on the trail of a ten-point buck. Then he made an astonishing leap and landed on the deer's shoulder. Before I could beat my wings three more times, he'd brought the buck to his knees and ripped out his windpipe.

I sat in one of the stubby pines watching the wolf tear into the deer. His ravenousness was terrifying. But I have to admit the speed and ferocity with which he'd made his kill had been breathtaking. I'd never seen anything like it. Soulless and earthbound though he was, he inspired a bit of awe in me.

Once he'd gorged himself, he sat back and started cleaning the blood off his snout with his long tongue. Most of the buck's carcass remained. It smelled delicious.

"You're quite the hunter," I said.

He lifted his head, looking surprised to see me. "We do better in packs," he said.

"Would you mind . . ."

"Help yourself," he grunted.

He was within striking distance of the remains, but I felt only mild nervousness about hopping down and digging in. Why would he want a mouthful of feathers with all that lovely meat around? And the fresh venison truly was delicious.

As I pecked away, the wolf yawned and looked up. The ravine had gotten dark, but there was still light in the sky.

"Maybe I will catch that nap," he said.

He circled a couple of times and lay down in the pine needles. It didn't take him long to fall asleep—hardly surprising after his skirmishes with the humans and chasing down a deer. After eating my fill, I returned to the stubby pine and looked down drowsily at the sleeping wolf, trying to think why I shouldn't accompany this amazing meal ticket on his journey.

4

THE SKY WAS AS BLACK AS MY TAIL FEATHERS when the
wolf and I woke from our after-dinner naps. He climbed
out of the ravine and headed due south. As we skirted a
ranch, a herd of cattle kicked up a fuss, but he left them
alone, and no humans appeared.

By daybreak we were in the foothills of the Beartooth
Mountains. Once we got to a good elevation, he did his
circling routine and settled down to sleep on the shady
side of a boulder. Late in the afternoon he got up and
chased down a hare. We agreed that it was a lot stringier
than deer, but edible. While we were relaxing after the
meal, I asked his name.

"Blue Boy," he said. "You?"

I told him, realizing a second too late that I'd missed a golden opportunity. I could have turned myself into something wonderful like a Miranda, or a Rosalind, or an Evangeline. Who could he have checked with? But at least he didn't snigger and say "Maggie the magpie."

For the next few days we made our way west through the mountains. It turned out I was good at spotting prey, and with him such a deadly predator, we had plenty of chances for after-dinner conversation. He wasn't very talkative, but I pumped him with questions, and using a little imagination, I managed to piece together his story.

The mountainous terrain gave him no problems because he'd grown up in the Canadian Rockies. He'd been the firstborn in his litter. This, it turns out, is a big deal to wolves. The firstborn grabs the nipple with the richest milk supply, giving that pup a big advantage over the others, turning him or her into a sort of heir apparent. But the life of a young wolf, firstborn or last, sounded even more hazardous than a young magpie's. Blue Boy's litter was six, and by the end of his first summer only two were left. All three of his sisters were killed—one by drowning in a stream, one courtesy of an eagle, one mysteriously—and one of his brothers wandered too close to the territory of a neighboring pack and got torn to shreds.

"My other brother nearly bit the dust too," he told me.

"How?" I asked.

"An owl."

"But he got away?"

"Almost wish he hadn't," Blue Boy said with a sniff.

This brother's name was Sully. When Blue Boy dispersed from his pack—his third summer—Sully came along with him. That next spring Blue Boy mated with a wolf named Bess, who whelped the five pups he'd mentioned. His last memory of home was going out to get them some food with his brother.

What happened, I now realize, was they were shot with tranquilizing darts and transported hundreds of miles south to a compound in Yellowstone Park. Coming to, they found themselves in a pen with collars around their necks. There were other Canadian wolves in other pens, but Blue Boy and his brother attracted the most attention from the humans. Perhaps it was their color. They both had the curious bluish tinge to their coats.

The first thing Blue Boy did when the tranquilizer wore off was to try to rid himself of the annoying collar. He couldn't scrape it off on the chain-link fence, however, and Sully wasn't able to gnaw it off.

"Maybe Bess'll do better," Blue Boy muttered. "Let's go home."

But when Blue Boy crouched to attack the fence Sully pointed out wolves in other pens who were doing just that, losing fur and teeth in the process.

"You have such great teeth, Blue. Why sacrifice them when you don't have to?" Sully nodded at a woodpile in a corner of the pen. "We can tunnel out under that."

Blue Boy had helped Bess dig a whelping den, but only because they'd been unable to find a pre-dug one. He considered digging to be for badgers. But he saw his brother's point.

They started tunneling after dark. The ground was marbled with roots and volcanic rock, but they kept at it night after night, trading shifts. Just before sunrise on the sixth night Blue Boy poked his head up between two pines outside the pen. He scrambled out, shook the dirt off his fur, and hissed at his brother, who'd conked out by the woodpile.

"Move it, Sull! The humans'll be up soon."

Sully stood and ambled over to the fence. "You go," he said.

"What?"

"I'm fine here."

"But don't you want to escape?" Blue Boy said incredulously.

"They bring us food every morning. And by the look and smell of this place we're an awful long way from home. It would be a killer trip. We'd probably get shot."

"But we have to get back to Bess and the pups! That pack across the river'll move in and slaughter them."

I later learned that the humans were about to release the wolves anyway. But, of course, Sully didn't know that. Like most of us at decisive moments, he had only his character to fall back on. He wavered a bit when Blue Boy's look of disbelief turned to contempt. Then the door of one of the humans' trailers slammed, and the moment was gone.

"He was always lazy," Blue Boy said. "That's why he stuck with me after we dispersed instead of starting a family of his own. But I never thought he was a coward and a traitor."

Blue Boy was definitely neither lazy nor cowardly. When we came to the end of the Beartooth Mountains, we faced a long stretch of open country before the next mountain range started, and ranchers took potshots at him as we made our way across it. But he rarely broke stride, his eyes trained on the mountains that would lead him home.

We were just coming into the foothills when a bullet caught Blue Boy in the neck. To my surprise, he didn't fall to the ground. All that fell was the aggravating collar. Amazingly, the bullet had severed it. The collar must have blunted the bullet's impact, for Blue Boy barely slowed down.

I'm pretty sure I crossed my first state line that day, passing from Montana into Idaho. Blue Boy picked up a scent and made short work of a deer. After dinner we both had a good sleep, and before sunrise Blue Boy got up and headed due north. But he moved less briskly than usual and left behind speckles of blood. The bullet must have penetrated his neck after all. Toward the end of the day he slumped down under a white pine without doing his usual circling.

"Does it hurt?" I asked from the lowest limb.

"Not much," he said.

The next morning I woke before he did. His wound was festering. I flew back to the deer carcass. Other creatures had been at it, and insects, too, but there was still some flesh hanging from the bones. I pulled off the biggest piece I could manage and flew it back to the white pine. Blue Boy was awake but hadn't moved. When I dropped the bit of venison by his muzzle, he sniffed it.

"Thanks," he said, and he ate it.

It wasn't much of a breakfast for him, but he licked his lips and rose to his feet and continued north. Around midday we reached the base of a steep, snowcapped peak. For me this wasn't a major hurdle, but most wingless creatures, even ones without festering bullet wounds, would have avoided such a grueling climb. To the east and west the terrain was considerably more hospitable. But Blue Boy was determined to keep on his northerly route, and he headed straight up the mountainside.

His powerful hind legs started to wobble and shake, but he struggled on. About halfway to the summit he collapsed. To keep his spirits up, I asked him about his home, but as dusk closed in around us his voice seemed to give out. My spirits sank. I'd thrown in my lot with this wolf, actually grown to admire him, and now he was going to die and leave me all alone in this craggy place.

But I was wrong about his voice. As a nearly full moon appeared between two peaks to the east, Blue Boy sat up and lifted his snout and let out a sound that made my neck feathers stand up. I've heard many wolf howls since, and they're always spine-tingling, but this one was so haunting, so melancholy, so soul-stirring that I swear the moon quivered in the sky.

It was only a matter of seconds before I heard my next howl: a small chorus of them, coming from far off to the south. I realized Blue Boy must have been calling for help. The howling went on for some time, back and forth, the other howls gradually growing louder, closer. The moon was near its zenith when it picked out three pairs of eyes on the edge of a pinewood downhill from us.

The glint of wolves' eyes in the night is a chilling sight. If I'd been wingless, I would have been terrified. Three wolves stepped out into the moonlight. Two were females who looked as if they might be related. The smaller, curvier one had a more lustrous gray coat and more flirtatious eyes. She walked by the side of the male, while the larger, sturdier female lagged a little behind. I liked the look of the male right off, for he had my color scheme: black and white, including a white blaze on his face. He was good-sized and probably would have impressed me if I hadn't seen Blue Boy first. As he approached, he growled, pulling his lips back to expose his fangs, and it occurred to me then that Blue Boy had howled not for help but as a way of putting himself out of his misery.

From my fox experience I knew there's a big difference between dreaming of ending things and actually facing death. But, unlike me, Blue Boy didn't shake or try to hide. He didn't as much as flinch. He just held the other male's gaze steadily.

"Ever seen such a big wolf?" the male said.

"Never," said his consort. "He's in bad shape, though. Look at his neck. Let's finish him."

I have no idea what got into me. As the couple crouched, their ears tilting forward aggressively, I dropped onto the ground in front of Blue Boy and squawked at the top of my lungs. The male wolf looked surprised. The female curled her lip, stepped forward, and gave me a swipe.

Her clawed foot knocked me sideways into a thorny bush. After a dazed moment I managed to extricate myself and aimed for a pine to gather my wits. I barely made the bottom-most branch.

"You hurt my wing!" I screamed.

It was horribly true. My left wing could barely flap. But the she-wolf wasn't paying the slightest attention to me. Her eyes were locked on Blue Boy's, as were those of the male at her side. The two of them snarled in unison.

But their attack was thwarted again, this time by the

other female stepping around and taking up the ground I'd held so briefly. She turned to Blue Boy, her whiskers quivering. Blue Boy bowed his head in resignation. Instead of sinking her fangs into his neck, however, she started licking it. As her tongue slathered the bullet wound, Blue Boy flopped down onto his side. She kept right on with her licking. Eventually she started nibbling at the wound. When she pulled her head back, a slug fell from between her teeth onto the ground.

She swiveled around to her companions. "This is the one they made such a fuss about in the compound," she said. "The one who dug his way out."

"So?" said the other two in unison.

"Four makes a stronger pack than three."

The other two didn't look convinced—though their ears had angled back a bit.

"You should find him some of your herbs, Frick," said the female who'd pulled out bullet.

The male snorted dubiously. But after giving Blue Boy a long look he trotted off into the darkness. When he returned, he dropped an uprooted plant onto the ground. The female who'd extracted the bullet chewed the plant up and spat some onto Blue Boy's wound. The rest she put by Blue Boy's snout.

"Eat," she said.

To my surprise, Blue Boy gave the green glop a sniff and ate it.

"I'm Alberta," she said. "This is Frick and my sister, Lupa."

"Blue Boy," said Blue Boy. "That's Maggie."

The three wolves followed his gaze up to me.

"Maggie the magpie," Lupa snickered.

I wanted to kill her. But she'd beat me to the punch. With a broken wing I knew I wouldn't last a week.

5

ON CLOSER EXAMINATION I wasn't so sure my wing was actually broken. But there were severely torn muscles. I could fly only a few feet at a time, and even on these short hops I veered disastrously to the left. With Blue Boy in equally dire straits I could only hope our ends wouldn't be too drawn out.

All that day Blue Boy barely moved, except for his heaving ribcage. The other wolves napped a lot, and at night they went off to hunt. At dawn Alberta brought Blue Boy back a chunk of deer meat. He lifted his head off the ground, took a few halfhearted bites, and passed out again.

The one called Frick evidently had a nose for medicinal herbs, and Alberta kept after him till he fetched a bunch. She chewed them up and applied some to Blue Boy's wound like a poultice.

"Won't help," said her brutal sister, Lupa. "He's lost too much blood."

Alberta spat out the rest of the herbs by his snout. "We'll see," she said.

"Anyway, he's not from the compound. He has no collar."

"It got shot off," I said.

"A likely tale," Lupa said.

She still had her collar—I wished it would shrink and strangle her—and so did Alberta and Frick. It seemed that, like Blue Boy, they'd been going about their business in the Canadian Rockies only to find themselves suddenly transported to pens in Yellowstone. After their release they'd left the park, too, migrating west into the mountains of Idaho.

Around midday Blue Boy came around, and Alberta forced him to eat the remaining herbs along with a chunk of deer. Once he'd finished, she asked what had become of his collar.

"Shot off," he said.

I gave Lupa a look, but she was preoccupied with her grooming—or pretending to be.

That afternoon, while the wolves were napping, I made the mistake of dropping to the ground for a peck of leftover deer. Try as I might, I couldn't get back up to my limb. The best I could do was scuttle onto a nearby stump.

When the three healthy wolves got ready to go hunting that night, Blue Boy astonished me by jumping up and saying he was joining them.

"You mustn't," Alberta said. "You need another day's rest, at least."

Blue Boy went anyway. This left me completely vulnerable, a sitting duck for any passing fox or bobcat or wolverine. But what could you expect from a wolf? I hunkered down in a rotted-out pit in the stump and tried not to move a feather. After first light a hawk drifted by high overhead, but luckily he didn't notice me. When the wolves finally returned, Blue Boy astonished me again— by depositing a nice hunk of venison by the stump. It was enough to last me a month!

Judging by how quickly Lupa and Frick curled up together and conked out, I figured they must have feasted at the kill site. Alberta lay down too but didn't close her eyes. The way she watched Blue Boy made me think he must have displayed his hunting prowess. After a while he met her gaze and said quietly:

"Will you do me another favor?"

"Another?" she said.

"You already saved my life. I was hoping you'd look after Maggie."

"Well, sure. But—"

"Thanks. I hope I can repay you someday."

Before Alberta could get out another word, Blue Boy turned and trotted up the mountainside. She sat there, stunned. I was stunned too. I couldn't fly after him, and by the time I thought of calling out good-bye, he was out of sight.

"Where's he going?" Alberta asked.

"He has a mate and pups up in Canada somewhere," I said quietly, feeling more doomed than ever. There was no reason in the world for Alberta to watch out for me while my wing healed. What was I to her?

We stared up the mountain for a long while. When Alberta eventually lay back down, she kept shifting positions, as if she couldn't get comfortable.

In time the other two wolves woke up. After giving her lustrous gray fur a thorough licking, Lupa looked around.

"This mountain's for the birds," she said, using a

turn of phrase I detested. "There's no water. Let's go back where we were."

"It's nice up here," Alberta said. "Don't you think so, Frick?"

Lupa gave Frick a sharp look, and he murmured that maybe going back south was the best plan.

When he and Lupa headed down into the woods, Alberta came and stood by my stump.

"Let's go," she said.

"Excuse me?" I said.

"You can't fly, right? I'll give you a ride."

Landing on the back of a steer was one thing. Cattle are torpid, slow-moving creatures with flat molars for chewing grass. Wolves, on the other hand, are fast as lightning, with fangs designed for ripping flesh—or feathers. I'd even kept a safe distance from Blue Boy.

"I'll be fine here," I said. "Blue Boy left me food."

"Don't be a birdbrain," Alberta said, using another of my least favorite expressions. "You're defenseless if you can't fly. Somebody's bound to come along and eat you."

And you won't? I thought.

"Listen, I can't split up the pack, and I can't break my word to Blue Boy either," she said. "So you have no choice."

She was right about my not lasting long on my own. And if she intended to eat me, at least it would be over quickly. But even so I would have balked if not for the look in her eyes. I know it's a strange thing to say about a wolf, but there was a real warmth in them.

Conquering every instinct in my body, I hopped onto her back. I clenched my beak, ready for the worst, but Alberta just trotted down into the trees.

I clung to her coat for dear life. When we caught up to the other two wolves, Lupa gave a snort at the sight of us, and I couldn't help thinking Trilby would have done the same. He'd considered a magpie and a bluebird a weird combination—what would he have made of a magpie and a wolf? But to my surprise Frick shot me a smile when Lupa wasn't looking.

The ride didn't get easier as the day wore on. We traversed countless ridges and several mountains. Late in the afternoon we arrived at what had evidently been their previous rendezvous site on a wooded hillside. Lupa gave me a hungry look when I hopped down off Alberta's back— none of us had eaten all day—but Alberta warned her sister off with a low snarl. The wolves napped a while and went off to hunt. I scrounged up a few seeds and berries and dragged myself under a bush.

When I woke at daybreak, the wolves were still gone. I hopped out into the open and tested my bum wing. It was no better. But when the wolves returned, both Frick and Alberta had brought back small chunks of meat for me.

The next day was much the same, and the next. As days turned to weeks, I tried not to dwell on the thought that my wing might be permanently out of commission, but I couldn't help resenting the wolf who'd turned me into a pathetic, earthbound creature. Still I had to give Lupa credit for looking good. When she wasn't sleeping or on the hunt, she was grooming herself.

At first Frick and I didn't talk much. But I came to realize he knew about more than healing herbs. He even paid attention to birds. He could tell a black vulture from a turkey vulture, and a Canada goose from a snow goose. One windy day he gave me a tip about putting pine sap on my feet to keep a better grip on my branch. Another day he showed me how the seeds in a Douglas fir cone look just like rats diving into a hole. Lupa rolled her eyes when he went off on one of his "silly tangents," but I took to chatting with him while she was busy grooming or napping. He was no Jackson, of course, but for a creature who'd been stuck on the ground all his life, he'd picked up a lot of information.

As for Alberta, she was so honest and dependable, I couldn't help liking her. She had a cheerful disposition, too. But one night—we'd been at the new rendezvous site almost a month by then—she woke me with a wrenchingly sad howl. I crept out from under my bush. There was no moon, but she was howling anyway.

"Are you feeling okay?" I said when she took a break.

"Sorry if I woke you," she said.

"What are you thinking about when you howl like that?"

"Well, I suppose I was thinking about Blue Boy."

Somehow I wasn't surprised. "He's quite a wolf," I said.

"I've never seen one like him. I don't think the humans had either."

"What do you mean?"

"When we were in that compound, they put us on machines to weigh us."

"What did you weigh?"

"I don't know."

"Do you remember the sounds the humans made when they read the scale?"

She gave an approximation. Thanks to my experience with cattle weighing, I was able to inform her that she weighed 120 pounds. It sounded as if Lupa weighed 115.

"When they put Frick on the scale, the needle went to the same place as with me," she said. "Most of the wolves were about the same. But with Blue Boy all the humans came to look. They weighed him twice."

She approximated the number, which sounded like 152.

"Isn't that amazing?" she said.

This probably explained what Blue Boy had said about the interest he and his brother had aroused in the humans. But I wasn't sure what to say. Size is a great paradox to me. Earthbound creatures all dream of flying, and flying requires lightness. I weigh less than half a pound myself. But these same earthbound creatures have an innate respect for bigness.

"I think Blue Boy liked you," I told her.

"He was just grateful I got the bullet out of him."

"I have a feeling it was more than that."

"Don't be silly. I'm not pretty, like Lupa."

Lupa's fur was shinier, and she had more sway in her walk, but Alberta was bigger and stronger. Frankly, I couldn't see that much difference between them—except for their dispositions. Maybe you had to be a wolf.

"I know it's silly to think about him," Alberta said. "But for some reason I couldn't help myself tonight."

Later that night, she and the others went off to hunt. They were still gone at sunrise, when a red-tailed hawk landed on a lightning-struck tree not ten feet away. His head swiveled toward me. He fixed me with his cold eyes and pushed off to grab me.

Next thing I knew, I was zooming away between two high-waisted firs. I zigged to the left, then soared up over the top of the forest. Hawks are fast, but they can't maneuver like a magpie—a healthy one, anyway. And I seemed to be back in the pink, my wing working perfectly.

I spent a gleeful hour doing aerial acrobatics. When the wolves returned from the hunt, I buzzed down into the same lightning-struck tree the hawk had used.

"You can fly again!" Alberta said.

"Good as new, thanks to you," I said. "All that fresh meat must have done it."

"Bravo," Frick said. "And now you don't have to feel bad, Lupa."

"I didn't feel bad," Lupa said. "She's just a bird."

But not even Lupa could put a damper on my spirits. I was actually grateful to her. I would never take flying for granted again. You have to lose something to appreciate its true value.

I was feeling so good that when Alberta's sad howl

woke me again late that night, I wished I could have shared some of my happiness with her. But she didn't need it. For there soon came an answering howl from far off to the north—a howl stirringly familiar to us both.

6

I DON'T MUCH LIKE FLYING AT NIGHT. But how could I resist?

There was only a light breeze, and a hazy moon silvered the tops of the gently swaying firs. After traveling several miles to the north, I spotted a pair of glinting yellow eyes moving along a ridge line. The ridge had clearly been logged, for the trees there were all saplings.

I must have gotten used to the other three wolves, for when I landed in Blue Boy's path, the size of this 152-pounder startled me. I don't know if I was scared or choked up at seeing him again, but when his fierce eyes fixed on me I lost my voice for a moment.

"I see your wing's healed," he said.

I bobbed my head up and down. "Thanks to Alberta," I said. "Did you find Bess and the kids?"

"Bits and pieces of them."

"Oh no! What happened?"

He clenched his jaw, not saying a word. They must have been slaughtered by the neighboring pack he'd mentioned, but he never spoke about it.

It was still dark when we reached the rendezvous site. The other three wolves hadn't gone hunting yet, and I think their initial reaction to seeing Blue Boy again was the same as mine. He couldn't have grown while he was in Canada, but he really was imposing. Alberta averted her eyes, but Frick held Blue Boy's gaze.

"It's good to see you," Frick said. "As Alberta's said, four's a better pack than three."

"Don't forget Maggie," Alberta said.

"Five is better than four," Frick corrected himself.

Lupa scoffed, but again she couldn't deflate me. I could fly again, and Blue Boy was back.

There was an awkward moment as to who was going to lead the hunt, but Frick quickly stepped back.

"He doesn't even know the territory," Lupa hissed.

Yet even she must have realized it would be a joke

for Blue Boy not to go first. And it was Blue Boy who caught the scent and gave the cry of the chase: the same bone-chilling cry I'd first heard on that split-rail fence back on the Triple Bar T. He may have been up for days, but he easily outstripped the other three. By the time they caught up to him, he was standing over a deer stretched out on a platter of blood-soaked pine straw.

After the feast Blue Boy led the way back to the rendezvous site as if he'd known this part of Idaho his whole life. While the other three lay down in their usual spots to rest and digest, Blue Boy sniffed around. Lupa shifted petulantly away from Frick, but when he moved next to her again she stayed put. As for Alberta, she didn't play games, didn't try to pique Blue Boy's interest by ignoring him. She watched his every move. And when he came over and lay down beside her, she let out a little yelp of pleasure.

They nuzzled and talked in low voices. Perched atop the bush I'd previously hidden under, I couldn't catch everything they said, but I did hear Blue Boy thank her for watching out for me. I felt a strange fluttering in my chest.

And so we made a pack of four wolves and one magpie. As winter approached, the wolves' fur got thicker and shaggier. Game became scarcer, and as soon as they'd hunted out one area, they would migrate east to a new camp. The wolves liked to hunt by night, but once they realized that if they waited till daybreak I could scope out quarry for them, they changed their habits. We began to sleep at night and head off at first light, with me leading the way.

I've since learned that in most wolf packs only the "alpha pair" mates. And no matter what Lupa may have thought, there was no question that her sister and Blue Boy were the alpha pair. But again our little pack made its own rules. When mating season came, both couples mated. In late April they chose a den site on the side of a mountain above a river, where both pregnant females dug dens. Having been stuck in a hooded nest for weeks on end, I sympathized with Alberta, and even with Lupa, for being cooped up. Blue Boy and Frick left food offerings on the thresholds. A week after the females disappeared, little squeaks came out of Lupa's den. I'd never seen Frick so happy. But even then he didn't venture inside to see the newborns with his own eyes. The very next day similar squeaks came from Alberta's den. Though Blue Boy had sired a litter before, he howled joyfully for half the night.

I have to admit I was curious to see what hatchling wolves looked like. But another week went by, and then another, and still none appeared.

"They've been out of their eggs a long time now, haven't they?" I said one day.

"We don't have eggs," said Frick. "They come out as pups."

"Then where are they?"

"Suckling," Blue Boy said.

Another week went by, and then, on the first really warm day of spring, everything happened at once. Lupa proudly ushered three pups out of her den—two males and a female—and barely a minute later Alberta came out of hers with two males and two females. One of Alberta's girls wasn't even half the size of the others, but in spite of having a runt, Blue Boy looked every bit as elated as Frick. The little fuzz balls were pretty cute, I have to admit, yapping and rolling in the dirt and spanking the ground with their forepaws. They didn't pay much attention to their happy fathers till Frick and Blue Boy knelt down. Blue Boy's litter toddled up to him one by one and touched the bottom of his snout with theirs. It seemed like some sort of sign of respect. When the other three pups went up to Blue Boy too, Lupa growled her disapproval, but Frick just laughed.

"Who can blame them?" he said.

Then another funny thing happened. The little runt went over and lifted her snout to Frick's.

"Poor thing," Frick said. "She won't last a week."

Even if they were wingless and soulless, these wolves showed more imagination in naming their offspring than my parents had. They named their firstborns first. Lupa and Frick's was a girl: Lucy. Alberta and Blue Boy's was a boy: Prince. Lupa and Frick called their other two Frank and Heather. Alberta and Blue Boy called their other boy Buster, and their girl Rosie. They didn't bother naming the poor, doomed runt.

The next morning was cooler and blustery. It was tempting to stay home with Alberta and Lupa to watch the pups cavort, but Blue Boy and Frick had pretty well depleted the game in the area and might need my help, so I went with them. After swimming the river and climbing a saddleback between two peaks, they still hadn't caught a scent. Flying on ahead, I spotted a pronghorn and zipped back to let them know. Pronghorn are elusive, so I flew above this one to give them a marker. But just as Blue Boy and Frick were closing in, I noticed a billowing cloud of smoke back to the west. I dive-bombed the two hunters, letting out a piercing shriek.

"You spooked him," Blue Boy said angrily.

"Get back to your dens!" I squawked.

Blue Boy and Frick raced across to the saddleback. From there they should have had a view of their dens, but the entire mountainside across the river was engulfed in smoke. They sprinted down to the river, leaped in, and churned across. I lost sight of them as they climbed out and dashed into the forest fire. I was beside myself. The wind was fanning the flames, and from overhead all I could hear was crackling tinder and snapping pinesap. Just as I was sure that all my wolves had been incinerated, one of them jumped out of the fire into the river. It figured it would be Lupa. But Alberta soon jumped in after her. And then, thank goodness, Blue Boy shot out too, leaping in farther upstream. The three of them swam to the other bank, and as they threw themselves onto dry land, I fluttered down beside them.

"Where are the pups?" Blue Boy gasped.

"I don't know," Alberta wailed. "They were with me—then everything was just smoke and fire."

"Mine, too!" Lupa cried. "And my beautiful fur, singed!"

"Where's Frick?" said Alberta.

We all stared across at the inferno.

"I'll go back," Blue Boy said grimly.

"It's hopeless," Lupa howled.

Before the howl died in her throat, Frick came catapulting out of the flames, his fur on fire. He splashed into the river and thrashed across and dragged himself onto the bank a ways down from the rest of us. Lupa let out a strangled screech of joy when she saw a pup drop out of his mouth onto the ground. But when we reached him we saw it wasn't one of hers. It was Alberta's runt.

7

THE RUNT WAS STILL ALIVE. So was Frick, though he was barely recognizable. The white blaze on his face was black, and his hindquarters reminded me of things I'd seen rotating on spits at barbecues back on the ranch.

He didn't seem to have any recollection of how he'd gotten so charred.

"I remember sprinting for the den and losing my way in the smoke," he said between gasps. "The heat was overpowering me when I heard a whimper through the crackling. The rest is a blur."

The only thing he was sure of was that if he'd stumbled on any pup other than the runt, he wouldn't have been able to carry it all the way back to the river. He'd just made it as it was.

I don't think this counted for much with Lupa. As the days went by, it became clear that she couldn't forgive him for not saving one of theirs. And though she tended to his wounds, I noticed she would keep her eyes averted. He *was* a sorry sight. The fur on his face and shoulders eventually came back as good as new, but his backside was permanently furless. And as the burns scabbed over, they looked worse than the raw wounds. All that was left of his once-proud tail was a stub. What's more, his hind legs had lost their spring. None of the medicinal herbs he was so skilled at finding did any good. There was no way he could hunt. So while the rest of us went after prey he was relegated to babysitting the runt.

With no bigger siblings to compete with for food, the runt gained weight and looked as if she would actually survive. Alberta named her: Hope. Hope was a modest little thing who didn't yap much. On mornings when my help wasn't needed to find prey, I stayed behind with her and Frick. I tried to draw Frick out, and Hope would sit listening to him with a rapt expression on her face, her smoky-blue eyes wide. I think she dispelled some of his gloom over his condition.

But the coming of another winter was really hard on

him. What fur he had thickened up, but his rear end had no protection against the cold. Even worse, Hope no longer kept him company while the others hunted. The forest fire had ravaged a vast territory, making game scarcer than usual, and though Hope was delicate by wolf standards, she joined the hunt. I know she didn't like deserting Frick, but although Blue Boy never spoke of it, losing his first-born son had hit him hard. I think Hope was trying to fill Prince's place.

When the hunters managed to make a kill, Blue Boy always brought a portion back for Frick, but Frick only picked at it. Not even needed to pup-sit, he fell into a deep depression. He perked up a bit in late February—the beginning of the wolves' mating season—but Lupa ignored his meaningful looks, and the light in his eyes soon guttered out.

Blue Boy and Alberta, on the other hand, were inseparable. But every ounce of their energy was devoted to keeping the small pack from perishing, and when spring came, they didn't produce a litter either. There were still blizzards in May. Even in June north-facing slopes were blanketed in snow.

One morning in mid-June I spied an antelope on the next mountain over. As soon as I gave Blue Boy the news, he bellowed out the call of the chase. Alberta, Lupa, and Hope answered with excited barks.

They felled the antelope in a clearing. While we were feasting, another wolf appeared, peering out of the shadows of the firs. Blue Boy narrowed his eyes and let out a menacing snarl. The stranger bowed his head and lowered his tail. He was only average-size, and his ribs were showing, but he had a sleek, charcoal coat. He had no collar, which made me wonder if it had gotten shot off like Blue Boy's or if he'd never been in the compound.

"You must be starving," Alberta said.

The wolf lowered his head farther and put his tail between his legs. Blue Boy sniffed and went back to his meal. The stranger crept up to the other end of the carcass and gingerly worked off a bit of meat. Blue Boy let it go.

After gorging himself, Blue Boy tore off a shank and dragged it away for Frick. The rest of us followed, leaving the stranger to pick the bones. Frick was lying listlessly under a rocky overhang on the next mountain over, but not even he could resist fresh antelope.

Their bellies full for the first time in months, the wolves were dozing off when the stranger reappeared just beyond the overhang, his dark coat agleam in the sun. Though clearly surprised at his audacity, Blue Boy must have decided the pack could use another hunter, for instead of attacking he rose to his feet and struck a lordly pose. The stranger came forward and did obeisance, touching his snout to the bottom of Blue Boy's chin.

"What's your name?" Lupa said as the new wolf sat down.

"Raze," he said, giving her an appraising look.

"Where are you from?" Alberta said.

"The Lamar Valley."

"Where's that?"

"The northeast corner of Yellowstone."

"You're young," Lupa said.

"Not that young," Raze said. "I'll be two in the spring."

"But you were born down here," Alberta said. "Don't you have a pack?"

"I dispersed last fall."

"Why?" Hope asked.

"I figured I'd find a mate and start a pack of my own," Raze said, giving Hope a dismissive look. "But I haven't had much luck. It was a rough winter."

"What's this Lamar Valley like?" Lupa asked.

"Like no place you've ever seen. Full of elk and prong-horn and mule deer."

"If it's such a paradise, why'd you leave?" Frick asked.

"Like I said, it was time for me to disperse."

"Elk, you say?" Blue Boy said.

"Huge herds," Raze said. "Bison, too. You could take down a bison, I bet. There's hundreds of them—huge things, and not that fast."

"How do they taste?"

"Delicious."

It was strange. I didn't know this Raze, and I'd never laid eyes on a bison, yet something made me doubt he'd ever tasted one.

"Maybe we should move there," Lupa suggested.

"Frick's not ready for a journey," said Hope.

"Go, please," Frick said. "I'd love a little peace and quiet."

"We couldn't leave you!" Hope cried.

Over the summer we moved base camp a few times but stayed in the general vicinity. Raze kept dropping hints about the game-filled paradise, however, and by September, Frick had gotten a bit stronger. One day Blue Boy took me aside and asked if I would mind checking out this Lamar Valley and reporting back.

I flew east the next morning. Blue Boy hadn't said anything about rushing, so I stopped whenever I felt like it to rest and chat with other birds. I passed over some rugged, snow-capped peaks and a big, turbulent river and an interstate highway. By midday I'd crossed into my third state: Wyoming. Soon after this I learned from a bunch of goldfinches that I'd also crossed something called the Continental Divide. I wished I hadn't asked what it was. They told me that on one side of the divide the rivers all flowed toward one ocean and on the other side toward another—which, of course, made me think of Trilby.

But once I was in the heart of Yellowstone the wonders there pushed even Trilby out of my thoughts. A great spout of steamy water shot out of the earth and nearly hit me in midflight. Not far away were bubbling hot springs, and mud pots, and what looked like giant anthills puffing smoke. There was a forest full of trees made of stone, and rivers working their way through canyons so deep that from the top even ospreys couldn't have made out fish in the water. There were pools that were orange or green instead of blue. Sampling one, I scorched my bill and shot off to a nearby lake to douse it. It was the largest lake I'd ever seen. Fishing in it were strange-looking birds with big yellow bills that stretched even bigger for storing their catch.

Most of Yellowstone was wilderness, but there were clusters of humans gawking at the wonders, and a few structures made of logs with peaked roofs. But what particularly interested me was a small compound in a clearing. Frick had told me about the place they'd been brought after they were captured in Canada, and this fit the description. There was an A-frame, three trailers, and a series of outdoor pens with chain-link fences. The A-frame had a garage attached with a dusty four-wheeler parked outside. A couple of humans were studying a sickly-looking wolf in one of the pens. The bigger human was a male with a furry face, the other a female with long hair the color of the wheat fields in Montana. When they went off into the A-frame, I spoke to the wolf, but he was ailing and wasn't in a chatty mood.

"Do you know which way the Lamar Valley is?" I asked.

Perking up a bit at this, he pointed his snout to the northeast. I headed in that direction, but by then it was almost nightfall, so I settled down for the night in a pine—a "lodgepole pine," according to a resident woodpecker. His hammering woke me earlier than I would have liked, but this turned out to be a good thing, for shortly thereafter I glided over a ridge in time to catch the sunrise over the Lamar Valley. A more beautiful sight I'd never seen. Trees lining a meandering river blazed gold in that first touch of sunlight, making a gilt frame for the deep-blue water.

Stretching to the hills on either side of the river were lush grasslands where herds of amazing beasts were grazing.

I landed on the bank of a pond and struck up a conversation with a duck.

"Actually, I'm a lesser scaup," she told me. "Though the 'lesser' is misleading."

She knew the names of all the valley dwellers. I recognized the pronghorns, but I learned from her that the deer with the big ears were mule deer, and the even bigger ones with the huge antlers were elk, and that the biggest, shaggiest creatures of all were the bison Raze had mentioned.

"I knew Raze hadn't tasted one," I said.

"Who's Raze?" said the scaup.

"A wolf from hereabouts."

"Oh, we love wolves," said a warbler from one of the gold-leafed trees.

"They're excellent providers," I agreed.

The warbler didn't know about that, but he claimed that conditions had improved for birds since the wolves' return.

"The deer and elk used to eat all the grasses we use for our nests, but the wolves keep them in check. This aspen I'm in right now would have been trampled by the buffalo if the wolves weren't here to chase them back."

"Buffalo?" I said.

"Another word for bison."

"This pond is thanks to the wolves," the scaup commented, pointing out the dam that had formed it.

"Wolves made that?" I said, surprised.

"No, beavers," she said.

She explained that when the trees made a comeback, so did the tree-loving beavers.

"I wonder if Raze is the young wolf who liked to look at himself," she said. "Is he black as a raven?"

"Yes," I said.

"Probably him. Summer before last, he'd hang out right over there." She pointed her squashed-looking bill at a place where the bank overhung the water. "He liked to look at his reflection."

"It must have impressed him," said the warbler, "because one day he went back to his pack and challenged his father. His father gave him a good smackdown and sent him packing. Haven't seen him since."

So *this* was what Raze meant by "dispersing."

"Have the wolves divvied up the whole valley?" I asked.

"I don't know, but I saw a battle between two of the packs," said the warbler. "The leaders had a vicious fight, and afterward the winning pack slaughtered the other one down to the last wolf."

"But they don't bother us," said the scaup. "My name's Sabrina, by the way."

"I'm Audubon," said the warbler.

Sabrina and Audubon! How could I tell them my drab name? But if my pack moved here, which seemed quite possible, lying would get me in trouble, so I divulged my name and lit out before they could make any snide comments.

The flight back to Idaho was nearly a hundred miles. There was a headwind most of the way, and late in the afternoon, when I arrived back at the rendezvous site, I was worn out. The wolves must have feasted on a kill that morning, for they were all napping—except Frick.

"So what did you think of it?" Frick said quietly, trying to whisk some flies off his scarred hindquarters with his nubby tail.

"Raze wasn't lying," I said. "About the valley, at least. It's full of game. Have you ever seen an elk?"

I was speaking in an undertone, but at the word "elk" the other wolves instantly woke up. And the very next morning the pack was on the move—to Yellowstone.

8

IT TOOK THE POOR EARTHBOUND CREATURES two full days just to reach the first big river. And then they had to trek well upstream to find a place to ford it without getting swept away. It was another day before we reached the interstate. The wolves waited till the dead of night, when fewer of the wheeled behemoths were rolling by, and dashed across.

The journey was hard on Frick, but he dragged himself along. On the afternoon of the fifth day we finally reached the ridge overlooking the Lamar Valley. It looked even grander than a week ago, the sun at our backs showing up the majestic peaks to the east.

"Did I exaggerate?" Raze said smugly.

Hope was agog. "I never dreamed such a place could exist."

"Blue Boy, look at the elk," Alberta said.

Blue Boy was salivating, but he insisted that we find a home base before thinking about hunting. Since Raze knew the area, Blue Boy let him lead us into the valley. However, Blue Boy wasn't cut out to be a follower, and when we came to a tributary of the main river, he barked for us to stop. Wolves prefer to settle near a water source, and he liked the look of the stream.

"This is Soda Butte Creek," Raze said. "But I know a better one."

Lodgepole pines seemed to be very common in Yellowstone, and as Raze led us north, I spotted the warbler, Audubon, in one of them.

"Maggie the magpie," he said when I landed on his branch. "Sorry, couldn't resist."

"I'm used to it," I said.

We chatted a bit, mostly about my recent travels. When I flew on, I found four of the wolves—Alberta, Frick, Lupa, and Hope—by another tributary off the main river.

"This one's called Slough Creek," Hope said. "Raze says it never dries up."

"He and Blue Boy went ahead to scout things out," Alberta said. "There's a scent post on this willow."

I'd landed in the droopy tree, but I didn't know what a "scent post" was.

"It's how we wolves mark our territory," Alberta explained. "But Raze says it's an old one."

"Smells fresh to me," Frick muttered.

I flew on upstream, gliding over a tree that had fallen across the current and landing on a big boulder by the side of the creek. Blue Boy and Raze were talking in the boulder's shade.

"Choice, huh?" Raze said, looking up a slope.

"Surprised it hasn't been claimed," Blue Boy said.

"It was. See, somebody dug a den. But now it's here for the taking."

Most of this side of the creek was wooded, but a grassy swath stretched from the boulder to the hilltop. Partway up the slope was a solitary aspen, and above that a hole that must have served as a den, and standing like sentinels near the top of the hill were a pair of lodgepole pines. It really was an inviting location, open and sunny yet close to the shelter of the woods, convenient to the game-filled valley yet a bit secluded, too. But Blue Boy didn't seem quite sold on it. He kept sniffing the air, his whiskers quivering. Then a howl made his ears shoot up. It was the sort of satisfied howl he sometimes gave himself on the way home from a successful hunt.

"Let's get out of here," he said.

Raze didn't budge. A moment later a pack of wolves came trotting out of the woods: five adults and four pups. The pups yapped excitedly, racing toward the den.

"Let's go," Blue Boy hissed.

"Scared?" Raze said.

This stunned me—and Blue Boy, too, I think. Before Blue Boy could react, Raze stepped out of the boulder's shadow. The ears on the adult wolves up the slope shot forward. The biggest of them, a black-furred alpha male, stepped to the fore, fixing Raze with a fierce squint.

"Back for more?" he said.

Raze took a step up the hill and snarled. The pups huddled together, whimpering, but the adults snarled back. The alpha started down the hill, a ruff standing out around his neck. Raze held his ground. I tried to will Blue Boy to get out of there.

He didn't. He stepped out of the shadow and gave the alpha up the hill the same level gaze he'd given Frick on their first encounter. But Blue Boy wasn't wounded now. The alpha froze. So did the rest of his pack. My mind raced. How could I have been so dense? In a flash I saw what Raze had been up to all along, since first coming across us last winter. It wasn't the fresh antelope that had kept him from turning tail and running when he saw Blue Boy—it was Blue Boy himself. He must have thought: now *there's* a wolf to get me revenge on my father! He must have been plotting to bring about this very moment ever since. The last card he'd played, accusing Blue Boy of being scared, had been risky, but clever.

Unnerving as it was to think of Blue Boy facing this pack, I couldn't help sympathizing with Raze's father. What a rude shock it must have been to see a wolf like Blue Boy emerge from the shadows! As my eyes flitted between the two alphas, a leaf blew off the aspen. It seesawed down through the air. When it hit the ground, Raze's father snarled:

"Off my territory."

I knew Blue Boy would never take an order like that. As he snarled back, all the wolves tensed up. But it was clear things would be settled between the two alphas.

When they attacked each other, the snarls and growls were so chilling I flinched and looked away. That was how I happened to catch the look of satisfaction that flashed across Raze's face.

9

WHEN I COULD BRING MYSELF to look up the slope again, Raze's father lay on his side with blood gushing from his torn throat. Blue Boy lifted his bloody snout and let out what must have been an instinctive howl of triumph. The slain wolf's companions gaped in dumb horror. I could only imagine their feelings at seeing their leader dispatched so swiftly. When Blue Boy lowered his snout, his eyes settled on them. They easily outnumbered him, even with Raze, but not one of them made a move.

Hearing something behind me, I turned to see Alberta rushing up along the creek with Lupa, Frick, and Hope in her wake. Even before they rounded the boulder, the other pack gathered their pups and fled. Remembering what Audubon had said about the winning pack slaughtering the losers, I figured that after what must have happened up in Canada, Blue Boy would be merciless. But he didn't give chase.

"Your old pack?" he said as the last of them disappeared into the woods.

"Sorry, thought they'd moved on," Raze said with a shrug. "But they have now. It's all ours."

"Your father?" Blue Boy said, eyeing the mangled corpse.

"He was a nasty old tyrant. I'll get rid of him." Raze snorted. "What's left of him."

As Raze dragged his father's remains into the woods, the other wolves came up the slope.

"What happened, Blue Boy?" said Frick. "Did that fool wolf challenge you?"

"Are you all right?" Alberta said, licking blood off Blue Boy's muzzle.

Blue Boy licked her back.

"It is a nice spot," Lupa said, surveying the slope.

"Look, Mother, there's a den already dug," said Hope.

All the traveling had worn Frick out, and he conked out as soon as he lay down. The others were hungry, but it was getting to be late in the day and they were weary, too. Hope and Lupa and Alberta found sleeping spots near the den. Blue Boy stood sentinel farther up the hill. I settled in the aspen. Raze spent a long time in the woods before rejoining the rest of us. I don't know if he was giving his father wolfish last rites or snacking on him.

In the pearly predawn light Blue Boy rousted everyone up. Frick remained at the den site while the others followed Blue Boy along a ridge trail in their usual hunting order: Alberta second, then Lupa, Raze, and Hope. I flew overhead. From a promontory overlooking the valley Blue Boy led the party down into the bottomland, aiming for a bull elk that had strayed from the herd. Blue Boy and Alberta circled downwind of him. The others stalked the elk from the upwind side. The elk lifted his imposing rack of antlers, sniffed the air, and bolted away from the stalkers—straight toward Alberta. She leaped up and clamped her jaws onto the right side of his neck. Blue Boy hit him from the other side. The elk tried in vain to knock them off with his antlers. He staggered a few steps, carrying both wolves, before stumbling to his knees. In a trice the other three wolves were on him too. It was a quick death.

The bull was my first taste of elk. I liked it. But the

wolves *loved* it. A grown elk is far bigger than a deer, yet the wolves managed to finish off half the carcass before a pair of enormous grizzlies lumbered up. Not even Blue Boy felt like tangling with them; he tore off a slab of meat for Frick and left the rest for the bears.

And so we established ourselves on the slope above Slough Creek. Food was so abundant in this northeast corner of Yellowstone that we didn't have to go hunting every morning. Some days the wolves just lolled around digesting the feast from the day before. Even when the snows came and Slough Creek froze over, there was still game to be had. The ousted pack never tried to reclaim their territory, and everyone felt the move had been worth it—except Frick, and maybe me. Frick's hindquarters were no more insulated from the cold here than in Idaho, and when mating season came, he had no more luck with Lupa than last year. He spent more and more of his time sleeping. Often he was still out when the other wolves returned from the hunt. As for me, with food so plentiful my game-spotting abilities were no longer needed, and I began to feel a bit extraneous.

On the brighter side, the snow finally began to melt, and as the creek swelled, so did Alberta's belly. Toward the end of April she disappeared into the pre-dug den. A week later we heard the whimpers of newborns. After depositing his chunks of elk meat in the den entrance, Blue Boy took to lying just outside, his ears pricked up. He was sure he could distinguish three different yaps. He started getting up well before the others to watch for the pups. Late one moonlit night in mid-May I woke to see him pacing outside the den as if the ground were on fire. There are places in Yellowstone where the ground actually *is* on fire, but here on the slope above Slough Creek the snow pack had only just melted, and there was still an eyebrow of snow at the foot of my aspen.

It was odd to see Blue Boy nervous, but I could understand his anxiety. He hadn't been lucky with offspring. He'd lost his whole first litter, and of his second litter there was only Hope.

"Think they're coming out today?" I asked softly.

"I can feel it," he said.

The other wolves were still curled up asleep. Over the mountains to the east the sky was still a rich magpie-black. A faint, triangular glow appeared—false dawn, it's called—then little by little the sky lightened to the nondescript gray of a catbird. Suddenly Blue Boy stopped pacing. Even from my aspen I'd heard the yap.

"Must be the firstborn," he whispered. "Sounds like a boy, doesn't it?"

I could understand his eagerness for a son, too: a wolf in his own magnificent image. As the rising sun began to gild the mountaintops, birds on the other side of Slough Creek started twittering—thrushes, by the off-key sound of them. Hope and Lupa stirred, and Raze, too.

All of a sudden a pair of pups stumbled out of the den. They were roughly the same size, a fluffy brown female and a mostly black male. When Alberta came out right behind them, Blue Boy barked happily and gave her a congratulatory nuzzle. The fuzz balls tumbled around in the new grass. Then two more male pups appeared—and one was riding on the other's back! The rider was a runt, his mount definitely the biggest of the litter.

Blue Boy shot Alberta a look of surprise. She shrugged. Blue Boy sniffed and knelt down. The first two pups wasted no time in toddling up on their little bowed legs and licking him under his chin. The runt slid off his brother's back and did the same. But the last pup got distracted.

"The firstborn?" Blue Boy said, eyeing him.

"Mmm," said Alberta.

A little downhill from the den a beetle with an iridescent shell had landed on a twig. The firstborn pup stepped tentatively that way, and the beetle opened his wings and took off. With a burp of excitement the pup chased it. He tripped and tumbled down the slope. If he hadn't bumped into my aspen, he might have rolled all the way down to the creek.

"Quite the little adventurer," Hope said. "What are you going to call him, Mother?"

"It's your father's turn," Alberta said. "I got to name you."

Blue Boy glanced down the notch, toward the valley. "How about Lamar?" he said. Then louder: "Lamar!"

The firstborn pup turned and clambered up the hill. But just when it looked as if he was finally going to pay his father tribute, the sun hit the creek, striking diamonds of light off it.

"This is the most beautiful place I've ever seen," Lamar exclaimed.

"Out of your vast experience of beautiful places," said Frick, who'd woken at the commotion.

The pup turned and fixed his eyes on him. "You have a thing on your neck like Mother," he said.

"A collar," Frick said.

"What are those little things?"

"Flies," Frick said, giving his nub of a tail a swish.

"What's this tickly stuff?"

"Grass," Frick said.

As Lamar bombarded Frick with questions, Alberta enlisted Blue Boy in helping name the other newcomers. They called the girl Libby and the boy Ben. Out of tact for Hope they even named the runt: Rider. Ben and Libby started sparring, as wolf pups are meant to do, and small as he was, Rider joined in. Lamar kept on grilling Frick about the novelties around him, oblivious to his father's narrowing eyes.

"What's the thing I hit?"

"A tree," Frick said. "A quaking aspen, to be precise."

"What are those things in the quaking aspen?"

"Budding leaves, mostly. The black-and-white thing's a bird."

"A bird," Lamar said, looking suitably impressed.

"She's a friend of ours, a magpie," Frick said. "Her name's Maggie."

Lamar's upturned eyes were an adorable baby blue. His body was mostly his mother's gray, but his face was an expressive mix of gray, brown, white, and black. As I was about to welcome him to the world, Rider let out a squeal.

Ben had cuffed the runt and sent him flying. Lamar raced over, helped the runt to his feet, and turned on his other brother, his tail shooting up. Ben's wilted.

"That's more like it," Blue Boy said under his breath.

The wolves spent the day playing with the pups. Watching the pups frolic, I noticed that none of them had any of their father's blue in their coats, but this didn't keep Blue Boy from beaming at them. Not even Lupa or Raze could resist them. By late afternoon the endearing little things were falling asleep on their feet, and Alberta herded them into the den.

Next morning I went off with the hunters, but after a few quick pecks of that day's kill I zoomed back to the den site. I made it in time for the pups' second appearance. Today Rider came out under his own steam, peering around hungrily. Alberta must have begun weaning them, for the other three pups came out looking hungry too. Frick had slept in as usual but woke up when Lamar started nuzzling his belly in search of a nipple.

"That's a dead end, I'm afraid," Frick said.

Lamar looked disappointed, but before long the hunting party returned, and Lamar and the other pups raced up to them and poked the corners of the adults' mouths with their snouts. It must have been wolfish instinct. The hunters regurgitated pre-chewed food onto the ground, and the pups dug in.

"What is this?" Lamar cried after gulping down a mouthful.

"Elk," said Blue Boy.

"It's the best thing I ever tasted."

"Out of your vast culinary experience," Frick murmured.

Libby and Ben kept shouldering Rider away from the food, but when the feeding frenzy was over, Lamar spat some up for the runt. I don't think Blue Boy approved of this—pups are supposed to grab all the nourishment they can—but he didn't interfere.

"Is elk over there?" Lamar asked, staring off toward the valley.

"Don't you worry about where it comes from," Blue Boy said. "Just have fun."

By "fun" he meant sparring. This was early training for the hunt. Lamar sparred with his brothers and sister for a while, but in time he got bored and tottered over to Frick.

"What are those tall things?" he asked, looking up the hill.

"Lodgepole pines," Frick said.

"What are the big creatures way over there with the spiky green fur?"

"Those are called mountains."

Lamar immediately headed toward the mountains, but his parents growled. Pups aren't supposed to venture far from the den. Lamar had to content himself with asking about things.

And ask he did. Ask, ask, ask. But at least he didn't repeat the same questions over and over. Once he got an answer, he moved on. And it didn't take him long to figure out who not to bother. He picked up on his father's disapproval of his questions, and Raze's annoyance, and Lupa's disinterest. He zeroed in on Frick—and me.

The height of the lodgepole pines amazed him, as did the sudden pageant of wildflowers. The sky amazed him too. One day it was the blue of his father's fur, the next it was the lustrous gray of Lupa's, the next it seemed to be full of the puffy white things, and the next it spat at us.

"Look, the birds can go up into it!" Lamar cried one morning.

"Those are just chipping sparrows," I told him.

I showed him what real flying looks like. When I landed back in the aspen, he was jumping up and down, trying to fly himself—a pitiable sight indeed. Not wanting to rub his nose in the natural superiority of birds, I pointed out that we couldn't howl.

"What's 'howl'?" he said.

He soon found out. One night in the wake of a hearty elk feast Blue Boy, Hope, Raze, and Lupa were keeping me up with their howling when Lamar's head poked out of the den. His little ears cupped at the sound of answering howls in the distance. I think this was his first inkling that they weren't the only wolves in the world. As he inched outside, he said in an awed voice:

"Look at the big yellow wolf eye!"

I think I was the only one who heard him. I was about to tell him it was called the moon when there was a different howl from far away, higher and more musical than the rest.

"What kind of wolf is that?" he asked.

At this the grown-ups noticed him.

"Why aren't you in bed?" Blue Boy said gruffly.

Lamar ducked back inside.

When Lamar and the other pups came out in the morning, it was sunless and cold. Blue Boy had gone off to patrol his territory, as he did periodically, but the rest of the hunting party was lolling around with Frick, bellies still full. Since Frick had slept through last night's concert, Lamar turned to Hope for information about the interesting howl.

"That was a coyote," she said.

"What's a coyote?"

"Scum," said Raze.

"What's scum?" Lamar said.

"Coyotes are something like wolves," Hope said, "only smaller."

"Especially their brains," Raze said.

"This from our resident intellect," Frick said.

Just as Raze was narrowing his eyes at Frick, Blue Boy returned. He stood a ways off, his tail straight up. Alberta went and kissed him under the chin. Lupa did the same, and Frick too, and even Raze. The pups quit sparring and followed the example of the adults, Blue Boy lowering himself a bit so they could reach. Lamar gave a shrug and for the first time followed the example of the others. Blue Boy let out a happy croon.

Later that day it snowed.

"What is this?" Lamar cried, dashing around in every direction.

"Snow in June," Raze grumbled.

"Can you fly in it?" Lamar asked me.

I flew off across the creek and circled back to my aspen. I think seeing me disappear into the snow gave Lamar an idea. He went to roughhouse with the other pups, and when Libby landed a clout on his snout, he pretended it was more powerful than it was and rolled off down the hill, figuring he could vanish into the snow as well and go exploring. He passed the big boulder by the creek and made his way along the water's edge. An interesting creature was nosing around on the opposite bank, a creature even smaller than he was, and when Lamar came to the log spanning the creek, he started across. But the log was icy, and he slipped.

Slough Creek is shockingly cold. I've rinsed my feathers in it. Lamar thrashed and gasped for air. I squawked for Blue Boy, who dashed down and yanked Lamar out by the scruff of the neck. Lamar coughed up some water and rasped a thank-you.

Blue Boy fixed him with a stern stare. "Just where did you think you were going?"

"I saw a coyote on the other side," Lamar said.

Blue Boy looked across the creek, and his expression softened. "That chipmunk, you mean? I applaud your hunting instincts, Lamar, but you're too young to leave the den site."

"I didn't want to hunt it. I wanted to hear that nice song again."

Blue Boy's expression hardened again. "One of my

sisters drowned in a creek like this when she was your age."

"You have sisters, Father?"

"I had three—but none of them made it."

"What happened to them?"

"They died."

"Died," Lamar said. "Why don't you wear a collar like Mother and Frick and Raze and Lupa?"

"I lost mine."

"How'd you lose it?"

"You ask too many questions, Lamar. At this point there's really just one thing you need to know. That the world's a perilous place."

"The world's a perilous place," Lamar repeated.

"And don't let Libby smack you around like that."

Lamar nodded, not mentioning that his tumble had been staged.

"You're the firstborn," Blue Boy continued. "You have to assert your dominance."

"What's 'assert your dominance'?"

His father sighed.

10

AS THE PUPS GREW, Lamar's size advantage increased. He was fascinated by every new flower that popped up, every new bird or insect that flew by, but he restrained his impulse to explore and even swallowed some of his questions, especially within earshot of his father. He did his best to "assert his dominance," too. The hunters began bringing back elk bones and hunks of real meat instead of pre-chewed fare, and Lamar would make a point of grabbing the biggest chunk. He spent more time sparring with his siblings, returning their swats with harder ones, and winning games of tug-of-war they played with sticks and bones. Strangely enough, the bossier he acted, the more devoted they became to him. All he had to do was press his ears forward and lift his tail for them to roll over and show their white bellies in surrender. But he wasn't despotic. The only thing he seemed to insist on was that Ben and Libby leave some food for Rider.

One day at dusk, just when it looked as if Rider might actually make it, a swallow swooped so close to the little fellow's snout that he went chasing after it. In a flash a short-eared owl dove out of the sky and grabbed him. Blue Boy raced after the owl and made a desperate leap, but he came up short. For a moment I was too stunned to move, then I shot after the beast myself. Magpies are smaller than owls, so my best hope was to harrass him into dropping the poor pup dangling from his talons. But he'd gotten the wind under his wings, and, fast as we magpies are, I couldn't catch up.

Finally, I circled sadly back to my aspen. Down below, Lamar was frantic. "What happened?" he cried.

"A hawk grabbed him," said Raze.

Catching my breath, I pointed out that it had been an owl.

"Hawk," said Raze. "Owls only hunt at night."

Blue Boy said something, but it was inaudible over Alberta's heartrending wail.

"What?" Lamar said.

"Maggie's right," Blue Boy said grimly. "It was an owl."

"Will the owl bring Rider back, Father?" Lamar asked.

Raze snorted. "When buffalos fly," he said.

Lamar, who didn't know what a buffalo was, looked up at me with his big blue eyes. "I hope that's soon!" he said. "Is the owl a friend of yours?"

"Heavens, no," I said.

"But Rider can't just be gone."

"Your fraternal feelings do you credit," I said, "but I'm—"

"What's 'fraternal'?"

"Brotherly."

"Inside!" Alberta cried.

As she herded Ben and Libby into the den, Lamar slipped off to the northeast, the direction the owl had gone. Blue Boy promptly brought him back by the scruff of his neck and shoved him into the den. Lamar popped right out.

"Rider always curls up next to me at night," he said.

"I'm sorry," Blue Boy said, with unusual gentleness. "I've lost brothers myself. But do you remember what I told you?"

"'The world's a perilous place.' How did you lose your brothers?"

It was remarkable. Even in his grief Lamar asked questions.

"One got killed by another pack," Blue Boy said. "The other . . ." His voice trailed off.

"The other?" Lamar said.

Alberta yanked Lamar into the den. Later that night she came out and joined Blue Boy in one of the most mournful howling sessions I've ever heard.

Next morning Lamar crawled out of the den before any of the adults were awake.

"Have you seen him?" he said, searching the horizon.

"I'm afraid Rider's gone," I said.

"Until buffalos fly?" he said, looking up at me hopefully.

I took a deep breath. "You shouldn't feel too bad. You were a good brother to him."

This didn't seem to comfort him much, but then he didn't have a lot of time to mope. As soon as Blue Boy got up, he announced that the pups were coming along to observe the hunt. I don't think he'd meant for them to leave the den area quite so soon, but he wanted to take their minds off Rider.

Everybody headed along the ridge trail, even Frick. Watching from above, I was afraid Lamar would pull a muscle in his neck, he was looking around so wildly at all the new scenery. When we got to the overlook, the hunters descended their usual winding path, leaving the pups with Frick. I stayed behind, too, curious to see Lamar's reaction to the valley he was named after.

"What are the shaggy giants?" he asked breathlessly.

"Bison," Frick said. "Also called buffalo."

"Can they fly?" The hope in his voice was heartbreaking.

"I'm afraid not," Frick said.

Lamar looked devastated. But there was so much to see that not even the thought of Rider could stifle his inquisitive nature for long.

"The smaller ones are buffalo pups?" he said.

"Calves, they call them," Frick told him.

"What about the ones with the branches on their heads?"

"Your favorite food."

"Elk?"

"Mmm. The branches are called antlers."

"Antlers," Lamar said. "And the ones with the antlers that aren't so branchy?"

"Those are pronghorns."

"What about the ones with the nice eyes?"

"White-tailed deer. The ones with bigger ears are mule deer."

Libby came over and joined us. "How come they don't eat each other?" she asked.

"They're mostly herbivores," Frick said. "They like grass."

"To eat?" she said, making a face.

"Aren't there any coyotes?" Lamar asked.

"It's mostly big game down there," Frick said. "Coyotes go for smaller things like mice and voles and rabbits. And wolf pups."

"*Wolf* pups?" Lamar said.

"Whenever they get the chance."

Silenced by this shocking news, Lamar focused on the grown-ups' hunting tactics. Till then, I don't think he'd seen his parents move at anything quicker than a lope. He sucked in his breath at the speed with which they headed off a bounding elk. Blue Boy struck first, sinking his fangs into the elk's neck.

"That's how you get dinner," Frick said.

He and I led the pups down into the valley, and we all joined the feast.

This became the new routine. The pups would study hunting tactics from the promontory and dine with the hunters at the kill site. In their sparring the pups took to grabbing one another by the neck, as Blue Boy had the elk.

It wasn't long before Lamar and Libby and Ben joined the hunt. Lamar was a natural. But if he'd inherited his father's hunting prowess he seemed to have missed out on his focus. One day Blue Boy spooked a fawn right toward where he'd posted Lamar, but Lamar had followed a bull snake over to the river to watch it go frogging. Another day, instead of helping hem in an enfeebled pronghorn, Lamar climbed a rocky escarpment to get a closer look at a mountain goat. Then came the day he stood spellbound on the riverbank, gaping at a wading moose while a fourteen-point buck galloped right past him.

Blue Boy may have chocked up these lapses to a young wolf expanding his repertory of possible quarry. But what excuse could he find for Lamar's habit of veering off the ridge trail? All it took was a frisky lizard or rodent to lure him off the beaten path. Sometimes Blue Boy actually went last instead of first, to keep an eye on his wayward firstborn.

Then came the day Lamar announced that he wasn't going on the hunt at all.

"Are you sick?" Blue Boy said.

"No. I'd just like to stay home with Frick."

Frick looked so pleased that Blue Boy actually let

Lamar get away with it. But the next time Lamar tried to play hooky, Blue Boy put his foot down, ordering him to come along. A couple of mornings later Lamar asked to stay behind again.

"There's plenty of food," he said. "You don't need me."

"In good times a young wolf has to hone his skills for the lean times," Blue Boy said.

"I'll hone my skills tomorrow," Lamar promised.

"You don't see your brother and sister shirking."

"Do I have to be just like them?"

Blue Boy's brow furrowed at this obstinacy. But it was clear that spending the day with Lamar gave Frick's spirits a much-needed lift, so Blue Boy grudgingly let his first-born take a day or two off each week. Lamar intrigued me enough that I broke my routine and stayed behind on those days as well. Or perhaps "unsettled me" would be more accurate.

"What do you think that owl did with Rider?" Lamar asked one rainy morning when he and Frick were sheltering under my aspen.

"Ate him, or fed him to the owlets," Frick said. "Life's about surviving."

"Is that all it's about?"

"Pretty much."

"How do those antlers help moose survive? They're so big and awkward-looking. Ben and Libby could sleep on them."

"They're probably to impress a female. Mating is part of survival—surviving into the next generation."

"Do you want to have another litter someday?" Evidently he'd heard about the one Frick lost in the forest fire.

"Nobody would want to mate with me now," Frick said.

"I'd mate with you."

"I appreciate the offer," Frick said drily.

The next time Lamar played hooky from hunting, he asked why his fur was getting thicker.

"Winter's coming," Frick said with a rueful look at his backside.

"How come everyone kisses Father under his snout?" Lamar asked, perhaps sensing that fur wasn't Frick's favorite subject.

"They're paying tribute."

"Why?"

"Well, your father's the biggest and strongest."

"Does that make him the best?"

"Pretty much," Frick said.

"But I wasn't better than Rider. And my father's no

better than you." Lamar looked around. "I don't think life's just about surviving, either."

You see why Lamar unsettled me? Even though his eyes were changing from powder blue to the same yellow as his father's, they seemed to take in things unrelated to just getting by. Attached as I was to the wolf pack, especially Blue Boy, I'd never thought of them as more than soulless, earthbound creatures.

As I'd learned on my first visit, Yellowstone had more than its share of interesting and beautiful sights, and on some of his non-hunting days Lamar would badger Frick and me to go investigate them. Both wolves impressed me with their interest in birds. I introduced them to Sabrina and Audubon and identified new species for them. My heart clutched the day we spotted a mountain bluebird. It wasn't Trilby, but this one was almost as resplendent, his plumage making Lamar's long jaw drop—proof that wolves aren't all colorblind, as some believe. I only failed him in his bird cataloguing once, when I got choked up and couldn't speak, but on that occasion Frick took up the slack.

"It's called a crow," Frick said.

Lamar was also intrigued by the mud pots and the petrified forest and the sulfur caldron. And he was wild about a basin of bubbling hot springs we stumbled on. But Frick didn't care for the smell of that place, so we didn't linger.

One day Lamar spotted one of the great waterspouts in the distance and insisted we go for a closer look.

"What is it?" he cried, stopping on a rise just above it.

Landing on some sagebrush, I told him what Audubon had told me: that they're called geysers.

"What are those things around it?" he asked.

"Humans," Frick said. The base of the geyser was ringed with them.

"They have so many different color furs!" Lamar said.

"I believe they call those clothes," I said. "The poor things don't have fur or feathers."

"Clothes," Frick mused, eyeing his naked backside.

"Humans have only two legs?" Lamar said.

I pointed out that there was nothing wrong with having only two legs.

"But they have no wings," Lamar said. "And why don't they notice us? We're upwind of them."

"They're not very sharp," Frick said.

I confirmed this. "You wouldn't believe the amount of food they waste."

"Though they did manage to get us here all the way from Canada," Frick said thoughtfully.

"I saw the place they kept you," I said. "Want to visit it?"

Frick shuddered. "No, thanks."

A few days after the geyser sighting, Lamar spotted a yellow-bellied sapsucker. Before I could tell him that sapsuckers are almost as mindless as blue jays, he chased it into a sun-dappled pine forest. Frick and I went after him. When we caught up to him, he'd forgotten about the sapsucker.

"It's thundering with the sun out!" he cried.

Frick sniffed one of the pine trunks. "We should turn back," he said. "There's a marking scent here."

Lamar kept right on going. Frick rushed after him, calling out that it was dangerous to trespass on other packs' territories, but Lamar didn't stop till he came to the brink of a yawning chasm.

"What is it?" he cried.

"I think it's called a canyon," Frick said. "Now let's go."

"What's *that*?"

Lamar was staring up the canyon at the source of the thunder: a river falling over a cliff taller than five lodge-pole pines stacked on top of one another.

"I think it's called a water—"

I shrieked. Four wolves were racing toward us along the canyon's rim. Frick and Lamar took off. They beat their pursuers out of the woods, but as they started up a hill Frick's hind legs began to buckle.

"Don't slow down!" he gasped.

Of course that's exactly what Lamar did. He stayed right at Frick's side. After they crested the hill, Frick lost his footing and slipped all the way down into a dry creek bed. As their pursuers came hurtling after them, Lamar dragged Frick in among some prickly pear cactuses. I strafed the attackers, squawking at the top of my lungs, but I confess I was amazed when they pulled up short of the cactuses.

Frick was lying in an exhausted heap. Lamar squared around to fight. The other four barked at them, front feet splayed, fangs bared—but they didn't attack. I landed carefully on a prickly pear and gave them another piercing squawk.

Once Frick caught his breath, he got up and ambled off down the creek bed. Lamar kept his eyes trained on the other wolves for a while, then turned and trotted after Frick. Pleased with myself, I gave the quartet of wolves one last menacing look before flying after my friends. The creek bed, or arroyo, made several twists and turns. After we'd gone a good distance, we stopped to rest.

"Thanks, Maggie," Lamar said.

"It was nothing," I said modestly.

"You think saving our lives is nothing?"

"You're a gallant bird," Frick said. "But we owe Blue Boy, too."

Lamar and I both looked around. There was no sign of Blue Boy in the vicinity.

"He sprayed a couple of those cactuses," Frick explained. "Those wolves smelled the scent posts."

"That's what stopped them?" Lamar said.

"They were from the old Slough Creek pack," Frick said. "They saw what Blue Boy did to their leader."

"What did he do?"

"I wasn't an actual witness. I think you saw it, didn't you, Maggie?"

"Let's just say it was over quickly," I said, feeling deflated.

For a minute there I'd actually thought I'd become formidable.

11

ANOTHER WINTER CAME, driving the tourists and the less hardy birds out of the park. But for Lamar the frost heaves and the pressure ripples on the icy lake and the snout-prickling air were marvels. He'd put on quite a bit of bulk—he was every bit as big as Raze—and his coat had thickened nicely. If his nose got cold when he was curled up at night, he simply covered it with his tail. He arranged a schedule for him and his siblings to take turns sleeping up against Frick's furless backside.

On one of his non-hunting days Lamar coaxed Frick back to the hot springs, convinced the place would warm Frick's bones. In the icy weather the basin looked like a gigantic steam bath, but Frick stopped stubbornly on the edge of the steam.

"Come on, the smell's not so bad," Lamar said.

"You go ahead," Frick said.

Maybe Frick suspected intense heat would trigger painful memories for him. But I followed Lamar in, and the steam felt good to me, even if visibility was lousy. Stumps, boulders, tufts of grass—everything was a blur till we were right up to it. We weren't the only ones escaping the cold. Lamar nearly stepped on a ground squirrel, which took off like a shot, and he terrified a black-tailed deer. Then a blast of wind cleared the air for a moment, and I spotted a pair of coyotes out ahead of us.

"Look at the funny little wolves," Lamar said, and before I could correct him, he called out, "Good morning!"

The coyotes shrieked. One bolted to the left and disappeared into the steam. The other bolted to the right and disappeared entirely, like a prairie dog into a hole.

"I didn't mean to scare you," Lamar apologized as the steam enveloped us again.

There was no response. Lamar felt his way tentatively to the right and came to a bubbling pool. He lowered his head and gaped. Something furry was floating there. He reached for it and pulled his paw back with a yelp. One of the coyotes had landed in the scalding water and been boiled alive!

Lamar fled the phantasmagoria in horror. I was right behind him. As we came out into the open air, Frick rose to his feet.

"You did some spooking," Frick said, amused. "You should have seen the deer light out of there—and that coyote. Must have been a nasty shock to see you." He paused, seeing the sick look on Lamar's face. "Did the vapors get to you?"

"A coyote?" Lamar said.

"A young female."

"A *coyote*? Oh, Frick. I think I killed one!"

"How is coyote anyway? I've never tasted it."

"I didn't eat him!" Lamar paced back and forth, his moist fur steaming in the cold. "I didn't mean to kill him. I thought they were young wolves. He jumped into a bubbly pool."

Beside himself, he dashed back into the steam.

I followed. There was no doubt about it: the unlucky coyote was dead. Lamar was crushed. A coyote howl was one of his first and fondest memories, and now he was responsible for a coyote's death. But on the way home Frick advised against mentioning his remorse to Blue Boy and the others. Mourning a coyote wasn't very wolflike.

It was Ben's turn to keep Frick warm that night, so Lamar curled up by Libby. But just as I was dozing off I saw Lamar get up and go over the hill. I flew soundlessly to a poplar sapling near him. There was a breathtaking view to the south: ridge after snowy ridge, like the white-caps the wind whipped up on Yellowstone Lake, lapping against great, jagged peaks under a nearly full moon. A coyote's howl broke the stillness, beautiful and sad, coming from the southeast. Lamar howled back. It was his first howl, I think—and I'd never heard one charged with such contrition. But all he got in reply was silence.

The next night Lamar took his Frick-warming shift. The night after that I was asleep in my aspen when I heard my name. I pulled my head out from under my shoulder feathers to see Lamar looking up at me.

"Could you do me a favor, Maggie?"

"What?"

"Find out where that coyote is?"

I could hear her howl. But as I've said, I'm not crazy about night flying, and I doubted very much Blue Boy would have approved of such a mission. However, he was curled up asleep by Alberta—and Lamar's upturned eyes were imploring.

The moon was so bright that it actually threw my shadow onto the snowy landscape as I flew along. I didn't have much trouble locating the coyote, on a rocky knoll a few miles away. She was perched atop a little cliff at the very summit, howling her poor heart out.

When I got back to my aspen, Lamar was right where I'd left him. I described the knoll, though I warned him the coyote probably wouldn't stick around if he approached her.

"But I have to apologize for what I did," he said. "What can I do?"

I thought a moment. "Most creatures respond well to gifts," I said.

He must have remembered what Frick had told him about a coyote's diet, for after the next snowfall he tracked down a weasel with snow-white fur. He caught a nice, plump vole as well. With both victims in his mouth he trotted off to the southeast before daybreak. There was no sign of the coyote on the knoll, but Lamar left his offerings in a shallow cave under the topmost cliff. Two mornings later he went back with a shrew and two mice. The earlier offerings had disappeared. It was impossible to know if they'd been taken by the coyote or another critter, but he kept making these errands for three weeks, always getting back from the knoll before the other wolves woke up. Blue Boy's territory was so secure that the pack didn't bother posting a sentinel at night, but one morning Blue Boy was up when we got back, awakened by the distant roar of a mountain lion.

"Where were you?" Blue Boy said, narrowing his eyes.

"I couldn't sleep," Lamar said, "so I went for a walk."

"And you?" Blue Boy said as I landed in my aspen.

"Just out stretching my wings," I said.

I was no more fibbing than Lamar was. He hadn't been able to sleep and had gone for a walk, and in following him to the knoll I had stretched my wings. But the little half-truth made me uneasy. Since throwing in my lot with wolves, my first loyalty had always been to Blue Boy.

Later that day, while the others were taking their post-hunt naps, Lamar managed to catch a rabbit, which he buried in a snowdrift. That night he was so exhausted, he slept in till well after sunrise, but the following night he went over the hill again. When he heard the haunting howl, he howled back. This time, after a long silence, the coyote resumed her howling.

Lamar raced back to where he'd buried the rabbit, dug it up, and carried it, stiff as a bone, to the knoll. He deposited his gift in the cave and retreated a short distance away. The snow glistened around him till a cloud covered the moon.

Soon a sweet voice came out of the darkness.

"You want to lure me down to kill me?"

"No!" Lamar said. "Not at all."

"Then why are you bringing me food?"

If she could make him out in the moonless conditions, it didn't sound as if she recognized him from her brief glimpse in the hot springs. I could understand his not wanting to fess up and turn that sweet voice bitter.

"Your howl sounded so sad," was all he said.

"If you're not out to kill me," she said, "would you mind proving it?"

"How?"

"By leaving."

Lamar left.

Two nights later he returned to the knoll with another offering—a creature he'd killed that looked like a weasel but with a bushier tail. He laid it in the cave and again waited a short distance away. There wasn't a cloud in the sky, and when the coyote appeared at the top of the cliff, her golden fur and delicate snout and shining eyes were plainly visible.

"I hope you like marten," Lamar said.

"I suppose I should thank you for the food," she said, making no move to descend from her citadel. "I haven't felt much like hunting lately."

"Where do you like to hunt?"

"This time of year Kyle was partial to the hot springs. Have you ever been?"

"The hot springs?" he said uneasily.

"If you go, be sure not to stay too long. The pools give off a gas that makes you woozy. Once we even saw a buffalo stumble to his knees. Kyle liked to pretend the gas had killed him and lie there like a corpse. One time a badger came snuffing up to him, and he grabbed it."

"Very clever. Is Kyle . . ."

"He was my mate. But he's dead."

"I'm so sorry," Lamar said.

After a while he asked her name, but she didn't reply.

"I'm Lamar," he said. "Where's the rest of your pack?"

"We don't have packs," she said, and with that she vanished.

When Lamar and I got home, he collapsed under my aspen.

"Oh, Maggie," he groaned. "She has no pack. Thanks to me, she's all alone. She has no one!"

I didn't say it, but it occurred to me that, in a way, she had *him*.

Two nights later he took her a field mouse. He retreated to his usual spot, and it wasn't long before the coyote appeared at the top of the cliff.

"My name's Artemis," she said.

Artemis! Another wonderful name my parents hadn't thought of. Lamar repeated it aloud, clearly enthralled by it.

"You're kind of a strange wolf," Artemis said, cocking her head to one side.

"Frick says I'm not very wolflike sometimes," Lamar admitted.

"Is that your father?"

"He's in my father's pack."

"The pack belongs to your father?"

"My father's the highest-ranking wolf," Lamar said, sitting up a little straighter. "Frick's . . . I suppose he's at the bottom."

"You're in a hierarchy?" she said.

He looked blank.

"That means some wolves are ahead of others," I told him.

"Oh," Lamar said. "Don't you have hierarchies, Artemis?"

"Coyotes don't believe in them," she said. "We just have couples."

The next morning Hope suggested Lamar go ahead of her on the way to the hunt, but he shook his head.

"It's time," Hope said. "You're much bigger and stronger than I am now."

"She's right," Blue Boy said.

But Lamar obstinately refused to go ahead of her. Artemis's views on hierarchies must have made an impression on him.

When I joined Lamar on the south side of the hill that night, Artemis's howl sounded a little less mournful, more like the musical howl we'd first heard back in June. But as he was about to howl back there came a crunching sound in the snow.

"Hope I'm not barging in," Frick said, casting a glance at me as he sat beside Lamar. "Isn't that a coyote?"

"Is it?" said Lamar.

"Not as yappy as most, but I think so. I don't suppose you know where she lives?"

Lamar hesitated before admitting he did. "Though please don't tell my father," he added.

"It's between you and me and Maggie," Frick said. "Do you know this coyote's name?"

"Artemis. She's the one who ran out of the hot springs. I killed her mate."

"Ah." Frick listened to the distant howl. "Did you apologize?" he asked.

Lamar shook his head.

"Well, I don't suppose it matters. After all, wolves and coyotes don't mix."

Two nights later Lamar took Artemis another vole. When she appeared atop the cliff, he asked if she thought it was true that wolves and coyotes don't mix.

"Of course," she said.

"Why is that?" he asked.

"It's a rule of nature."

"Couldn't we be friends?"

"You want me to be friends with a wolf?"

"Well, with me. Though . . ."

"Though what?"

After studying the snow at his feet for some time, Lamar blurted out, "I'm the one who accidentally scared you and Kyle at the hot springs. I'm so sorry."

He must have decided that apologizing did matter. Or maybe living a lie had eaten away at him. But when he lifted his eyes Artemis was gone.

The next night he returned her howl, but she didn't

answer. Two nights later he took her a shrew. He waited till dawn, but she never appeared at her cliff top. Night after night Lamar took her offerings and waited hopefully for her to appear. But it was always some other creature—an eagle or a badger or a raven—that eventually showed up and grabbed the food.

Finally Lamar went three straight nights without taking her anything. On his next non-Frick-warming night he slipped away from the others and slumped under my aspen.

"No more trips to the knoll?" I said.

"It's not fair to her," he said forlornly. "If I go, she stays away. It's her home."

The leafless aspen was swaying gently, but after a while the breeze died away. Lamar stared off into the distance, his ears cupped. All was snow-muffled silence till a sigh escaped him.

I was stunned by the pinch that quiet sigh gave my heart.

12

IT WAS ALMOST AS IF THERE WAS A SIMILARITY, some real connection, between me and this wolf. It was a disconcerting thought. Blue Boy's prowess and power were awe-inspiring, and Frick's breadth of knowledge was surprising, but I never imagined I'd experience a feeling of actual kinship with a wingless creature. Yet something about this young wolf yearning for a coyote reminded me of myself when I was younger. Though, in fact, Lamar's situation was bitterer than mine had ever been. I'd been bored with my mate and deserted him; Lamar had unintentionally murdered Artemis's.

While Lamar was suffering from unrequited love, his

parents were like a couple of lovebirds. Even while stalking prey, Blue Boy hardly left Alberta's side. One day they actually played a game of tag on our slope. Blue Boy was usually "it," and when Alberta caught him, she would give him a slathering with her tongue.

"Mating season," Frick explained, eyeing Lupa wistfully.

Raze was eyeing Lupa too—more suggestively than wistfully. Lupa acted oblivious, but she did catch Raze's eye for a moment.

Raze moved his sleeping spot nearer to Lupa's. One evening he scooted so close their tails touched. She pulled hers back. At around midnight Raze tried to snuggle up to her. She shifted away. He gave her a nudge and walked down the slope, away from the other sleeping wolves. For a while Lupa stayed put, but eventually she got up, shook the snow off her fur, and meandered down to where he was. This was very near my aspen, but I doubt they gave me a thought. I barely existed to either of them.

"Don't you like me?" Raze said in an undertone.

"Only the alphas can mate," she said.

"I heard different."

"We were a ragtag bunch then, hardly a pack."

"What if we took off and started a pack on our own?"

"Just the two of us? We'd never make it."

Lupa went back up the hill, though not without a little extra sway in her walk. When she settled down in the snow, Raze's gaze shifted to Libby and Ben. It was Lamar's night to warm Frick, so Libby and Ben were curled up together.

I suspected he was thinking of wooing them to join his new pack, but with Libby he never got the chance. In early March, temperatures soared above freezing, and one day, on her way across the Lamar River, she broke through the ice. It was even quicker than with Rider. One second Libby was there—the next second she was gone forever.

Everyone was distraught, especially her mother. But at least Alberta had something to distract her from her sorrow, for she couldn't long hide the fact that a new litter was on its way. Ben, on the other hand, seemed truly lost. I'd been so taken with Lamar that I hadn't paid much attention to his siblings, but no one could have missed how inseparable Ben and Libby had been. Now Ben had no one to play or spar with. When Lamar offered to spar with him, Ben muttered that it wouldn't be a fair contest; Lamar was so much bigger. Hope did her best to pay more attention to him, but then tragedy struck *her*. The warm snap was just a tease, and when temperatures plummeted again, everything turned very icy. One morning, on the way down the path from the overlook, Hope lost her footing and slipped all the way to the bottom, impaling herself on a branch jutting out of a fallen tree. The other hunters were well out ahead, leaving only Lamar and Ben to race down and pull her off. The puncture wound was near her heart.

"Take her back to Frick," I cawed, remembering how he'd saved her when she was a tiny thing.

Ben helped sling her across Lamar's back, and Lamar carried her home. Hope was panting so heavily that I was afraid she was breathing her last, but when Lamar gently deposited her in the snow near the den she managed to speak.

"You're good"—she gasped —"at carrying runts."

Frick was sleeping in, as he always did on days when Lamar went on the hunt, but the sight of Hope's serious wound transformed him. He sprinted into the woods. I'd never seen him move so fast. He came racing back, slid to his knees by Hope, and gave her what looked like a long kiss.

"Chew," he said when he broke away.

Hope chewed. Leafy bits leaked out of her mouth. Frick must have dug up some healing herbs he'd buried in the woods and transferred them from his mouth to hers.

Frick nursed her through the dangerous phase. But it was clear she was going to be out of action a while, and with another hunter lost and game growing scarcer and scarcer Lamar got no more days off. He didn't get any nights off from Frick-warming, either. Raze had suddenly taken Ben under his wing—if you can use such an expression with wolves—and the grateful young wolf insisted on sleeping by his new mentor.

As things got worse, the wolves went back to their old habit of hunting at night. Much as I disliked it, I went with them, but they had no more luck in the dark than they'd had in the daylight, and I was glad when they lapsed back to their morning schedule.

The first thing Hope did when she was on her feet again was suggest to Lamar that *she* take over Frick-warming duties.

"The truth is, I need warming myself," she said, averting her eyes shyly. "Part of my recovery."

With April as cold as January, Hope and Frick took to sleeping so closely entwined they seemed like one wolf. Lamar was free again to slip over the hill at night and listen for Artemis. But although there were plenty of wolves howling, and the odd coyote, Artemis's musical howl was missing.

Lamar pinned his hopes on the next full moon. And it turned out to be such a lovely, clear night that, perched near him in the poplar sapling, I almost felt like howling myself. But Artemis didn't.

"What can it mean, Maggie?" he asked anxiously.

I figured she'd either been killed or found a new mate, but I didn't have the heart to share my theories.

"Maybe she has laryngitis," I said.

This idea cheered him up, but only briefly. "She couldn't have had it *this* long," he said.

His doleful expression was hard to take, so I set my misgivings aside and flew off into the night. The moon was bright, visibility excellent. When I got to the knoll, I flew around to the far side and spotted Artemis curled up alone under a snowy bough.

I zipped back to Lamar and reported that she was semi-hibernating.

"Oh, thank you!" he cried.

The next morning Lupa took Hope aside.

"You have a sweet nature, Hope," Lupa said.

"Thank you," Hope said.

"But a wolf can carry sweetness too far. I realize Frick nursed you back to health. But if you want to show your gratitude it's enough to listen to his yammering. Just because you're wispy and don't have a very lustrous coat doesn't mean you have to settle for cuddling with a monstrosity."

"I don't think he's monstrous at all," Hope said. "But I know you used to be a couple. If it upsets you that—"

"Good heavens, no!" Lupa cried.

When Hope and Frick cuddled up that evening, Lupa gave Raze a look out of the corner of her eye. He ignored it. He ignored it the next night, too. Maybe he was playing it cool because she'd wounded his pride by turning him down earlier.

In the middle of the month snow fell day after day without a break. Hunting was impossible. I braved the blizzard for a couple of trips to the dump behind the Old Faithful Snow Lodge, where humans came even in the winter. As for the wolves, they just loafed around conserving their energy—though one afternoon they all suddenly sat up, their whiskers quivering alertly. A moment later my aspen shivered. In fact, everything shivered: the lodgepole pines, even the snowy ground.

"What is it?" Lamar said.

"An earthquake," said Frick.

There were two aftershocks. But eventually the wolves

settled down, and the snow kept falling monotonously. As the days went by, everyone got scrawnier except Alberta.

By the time a sunny morning finally came, Alberta was too pregnant to go on the hunt, so she stayed home with Frick. I went off with the others. From the promontory it looked as if a puffy white quilt had fallen over the Lamar Valley. There was no trace of the river, and the late snowstorm had driven even diehard elk, deer, and pronghorns south. The only creatures in sight were buffalo swaying their great, shaggy heads back and forth, trying to clear away snow to get to the meager grass underneath.

"Looks like bison or nothing," Raze said.

"You've felled them before?" Blue Boy said.

"Sure."

I just knew this was a whopper. After telling it, Raze pointed out a big bull standing apart from the others, his nostrils snorting great clouds of breath sideways in the frozen air. Raze suggested Lupa, Lamar, and Ben approach their target from upwind while he and Blue Boy station themselves downwind. The newly fallen snow hadn't crusted over, and Lamar sank in so deep I doubt he saw what happened. I did, of course. The bull smelled the three approaching from upwind and plowed off in the other direction, according to plan. Then Blue Boy leaped onto his shaggy neck. But Raze didn't. The buffalo snorted angrily and gave his mighty horns a shake, sending Blue Boy flying.

As the buffalo plodded off to join his herd, I shot down near where Blue Boy lay. The snow around him was turning crimson. I let out a horrified squawk, and the wolves quickly converged on him.

"Sorry," Raze said. "I slipped."

"Did his horn get you, Father?" Lamar cried.

"Just grazed me," Blue Boy muttered.

It looked to me as if the buffalo had gored him badly, but Blue Boy ignored Lamar's offer to carry him. He made it back to camp under his own steam, though he left a trail of blood in the snow. Alberta took one look at him and did something unheard of. She herded him into the whelping den. The sun disappeared along with them, and soon snowflakes were falling again.

"Just what we needed," Lupa said wearily.

"Do you think Father will be all right?" Hope said, hoarse with concern.

"Not for a while anyway," Lupa said.

"Let's just hope another alpha doesn't come sniffing around," Frick said.

Hope sucked in her breath.

"That could be problematic, huh?" Raze said thoughtfully.

"Very problematic," said Ben, though I doubt he knew what the word meant.

"Do you think something to eat would help Father?" Lamar asked.

"The only food around is buffalo," Hope said grimly.

But Lamar had experience catching smaller game. Though he'd done most of his hunting for Artemis by the creek, the notch was so chock-full of snow that he would have had to be a snowshoe hare to negotiate it now, so he headed along the wind-scoured ridge trail. I didn't spot a thing as I flapped overhead, but wolves don't have such long noses for nothing, and he soon caught a scent. He was weaving along with his snout to the ground when I let out a warning squawk. A strange wolf was standing in the trail ahead of him.

Lamar's ears shot back in alarm. I dropped onto an icy rock to get a steadier look at the stranger. He was an adult male, but I was pretty sure he wasn't the marauding alpha Frick feared. Even with a mantle of snow he was smaller than Lamar. He looked underfed—he had on a collar that was quite loose on his neck—and where his left ear should have been there was just a raw wound.

"Am I trespassing?" he said, his tail held low.

"You're on our territory," said Lamar.

"I thought I got a whiff of Blue Boy's marking scent."

"You know Blue Boy?" I said.

The stranger's quizzical look reminded me that magpies didn't normally consort with wolves. "Blue Boy's my brother," he said.

Lamar's eyes widened. "Really?"

"Name's Sully," the wolf said, giving himself a shake. His dusting of snow flew off, revealing a coat exactly the same bluish color as Blue Boy's. This had to be the brother Blue Boy had called a traitor and a coward. But, of course, Lamar didn't know that. And I couldn't very well tell him in front of Sully.

"If you're Blue Boy's brother, you'd be my uncle," Lamar said.

"If you're Blue Boy's son," Sully said, "and by your size I'd guess you are. What's your name?"

Lamar had gotten distracted by the ugly wound where the ear should have been, but when Sully asked again Lamar answered.

"Do you think your father would take another wolf into his pack, Lamar?" Sully said.

"It must be fate," Lamar declared as a gust of wind blew snow across the trail. "We're down to only four hunters. My father . . . your brother just got hurt."

"Not badly, I hope," Sully said.

"A buffalo got him with his horn."

"Ouch."

"Looks like somebody got you, too," Lamar said. "Frick might be able to help you."

Lamar led his newfound uncle back along the ridge. As we approached the den, Raze stood up and growled. Ben mimicked him, though his growl wasn't very menacing.

"This is Blue Boy's brother, Sully," Lamar announced.

"What a ghastly wound," Lupa said, making a face. "What happened to you?"

"A little accident," Sully said.

Just as I landed in my aspen, Blue Boy emerged from the den. Injured though he was, he rose to his full height, his tail and ears going straight up.

"Hullo, Blue Boy," Sully said. "It's been a long time."

"What do you want?" Blue Boy said icily, his yellow eyes slits.

"I was hoping maybe . . . Could I join up with you?"

Blue Boy snorted a plume of vapor into the snowy

air. Sully flopped onto his belly, his ear pressed back flat against his head.

"Please?" he begged. "I don't have anywhere else to go."

Lamar winced at the sight of his uncle groveling. As for Blue Boy, I don't think I'd ever seen him look so contemptuous.

"Get out of here," he snarled.

13

ALBERTA HAD NEVER COME OUT OF THE DEN, and as Sully slinked off into the blizzard, Blue Boy rejoined her, leaving behind a red splotch on the packed snow.

"Was that really our uncle?" Hope said.

"Hard to believe someone so spineless could be related to your father," Frick said. "But judging by his coat, I'd say yes."

"Mangy-looking beggar," Raze said. "Good riddance."

"Good riddance," said Ben, like an echo.

"But couldn't we use another hunter?" Hope said.

I'm not sure Lamar heard what the others were saying. He seemed to be in shock. The den was supposed to be off-limits now that he was grown, but he ignored the unwritten law and went in anyway.

It wasn't a long visit, and he didn't come out looking happy.

"Was that wolf our uncle?" Hope asked.

Lamar grunted.

"Why was Father so mean to him?"

Instead of answering, Lamar started pacing, much as Blue Boy had done the day of Lamar's first appearance. As the sky darkened, the snow let up, and all the wolves except Lamar curled up for the night.

Eventually Lamar came down under my aspen. "You never met my uncle before, Maggie?" he asked quietly.

"No," I said. "What happened in the den?"

He sniffed.

"What did you say to your father?"

"I asked if he had no fraternal feeling. He said it wasn't my concern. I don't understand it, Maggie. If Rider came back . . ."

He stared off to the northeast, the direction the owl had taken his little brother. I imagined his squeals of delight if Rider somehow reappeared, and saw how Blue Boy's reaction to *his* little brother's reappearance might seem heartless. Of course, he didn't know what Blue Boy had told me about Sully refusing to go back to Canada to help protect his family. But I figured if Blue Boy wanted him to know about that, he would have told him.

Now Lamar started pacing under my tree. He wore a track in the snow. When a few stars started twinkling between dispersing clouds, he made his way slowly up the slope to where Frick and Hope were lying together.

"I wanted to say good-bye," Lamar said.

They both sat up abruptly.

"You're not leaving the pack?" Frick said, sounding shocked.

"You're not even a year old yet!" Hope said.

Lamar gave them a steady gaze. "I think it's time."

"You'd leave with our father hurt and everyone starving?" Hope asked.

This must have made an impression, for Lamar walked a ways off and settled down for the night.

In the morning the sun came out, and so did Blue Boy. He looked a little wobbly as he stood outside the den, but his tail was proudly erect.

"You can hunt?" Raze said, eying him cagily.

"You mustn't, Father," said Hope.

"There's no point in anyone going," Lupa said

matter-of-factly. "There's only buffalo, and if Blue Boy can't bring one down, no one can."

"I know where we might find a more manageable one," Lamar said.

Hope turned to him. "Where?"

"The hot springs. I heard buffalo sometimes go there to feed and get woozy from the gas."

"You're woozy from gas," Raze said.

"Yeah, you're woozy from gas," Ben said.

But Blue Boy looked interested. "Where'd you hear this, Lamar?"

When Lamar hesitated, I said:

"From me. When buffalo come out of the steam, they're as clumsy as ducks out of water."

"Bird blathering," Raze said.

Before I could retort, Frick got up off his scabrous rump. "Let's go," he said.

He spoke so crisply, it made me wonder if Hope's company had given him a shot of confidence. Blue Boy actually followed him. Raze remained at the den site, as did Ben, but the rest of us went along.

When we got to the edge of the hot springs basin, Hope stayed behind with Frick and Alberta while Blue Boy, Lupa, and I followed Lamar into the steam. It was like going from winter to summer in a blink. The steam wasn't quite as thick as last time, and creatures fell over themselves to get out of the wolf pack's way—except for one. Munching on a mound of grass between two sulfurous pools stood a buffalo as big as the one who'd gored Blue Boy.

Lupa hit him first, landing on the beast's neck a second before Lamar hit his flank. With a grunt of surprise the buffalo lifted his head and shook it, but without much vigor. Blue Boy, even in his weakened state, wasn't far behind, going for the legs. The beast heaved himself a few steps forward, then let out a bewildered whinny and sank to his knees.

The throat was so shaggy Lupa had trouble locating the windpipe, but she did. The buffalo had barely gurgled his last when she dug into his midsection.

"Not here," Lamar said.

Lupa looked up with blood drooling down her chin— the first time I'd ever seen her in disarray. She must have been truly famished.

"The gases," Lamar said. "That's what made him so sluggish."

Blue Boy instructed them to tear off the biggest chunks they could and drag them out to the others. This required numerous trips. By the last, the three of them had to sit and gulp down breaths of the fresh air before they were clearheaded enough to tackle the task of dragging the butchered buffalo home. Blue Boy's wound had reopened, and Alberta was so fiercely against his doing more work that he actually obliged her, letting Frick take his place on the next leg. It was a toilsome, messy job. By the time the wolves got the meat to the whelping den, they were soaked with blood.

At the sight of the haul Raze retreated churlishly to the hilltop with Ben shuffling behind him. Spiteful as Raze was, I felt a prick of pity for him. Being proven wrong is a bitter pill—especially on an empty stomach, with the smell of fresh meat in the air.

Blue Boy gave Alberta the most succulent hunk of meat and claimed the juiciest of the remaining pieces for himself. Lupa picked out a prime chunk. Hope tried to get Lamar to go next, but he waited till she and Frick had served themselves before joining the feast. I perched on the liver and took dainty pecks. It was sublime.

The pile of buffalo meat looked big enough to last us till the weather improved and elk returned to the valley, so I figured Lamar could now leave the pack with an easy conscience. But it was getting toward nightfall, and he'd barely swallowed his last bite when a full stomach and the grueling day knocked him out. Frick didn't last much longer. Lugging the meat from the hot springs was the most exertion he'd put out since the trek from Idaho. Hope passed out too, her chin on Frick's scarred haunch. Blue Boy kicked some snow over their provisions before curling up next to Alberta by the entrance to the den. Lupa sat eyeing the cuddly spectacle of Hope and Frick with disgust. But at moonrise her gaze shifted up the hill to Raze. He was awake, but he ignored her, so it surprised me when she grabbed a hunk of meat and carried it up the snowy slope.

14

LAMAR WOKE BEFORE THE SUN. Up the hill Lupa was sleeping by Raze, with Ben not far off, while the other wolves lay curled up around our new larder. Lamar picked out a juicy piece of buffalo meat, and I followed him to the rocky knoll. He left his offering in the shallow cave at the foot of the cliff and retired to his old spot.

In the course of the morning I got distracted several times: by the sun hitting the snowcapped mountaintops to the south, by the glint of a curved horn on a bighorn sheep on a smaller mountain nearby, by a flock of cranes flying by with their long, spindly legs pressed together behind them like rudders. But I don't think Lamar's eyes ever left the cliff top. The afternoon grew quite warm, and at one point I flew around to the back of the knoll and saw Artemis sitting up under her bough, sniffing the air. Not wanting to miss Lamar's reaction when she made her appearance, I flew back to the other side. But she didn't appear. Lamar kept his vigil till late that night, when he could no longer keep his eyelids from drooping shut.

Only then did Artemis show up. I wanted to wake Lamar, but the look the coyote gave me made me hold my tongue. She came down and ate about half the raw buffalo steak, then took the leftovers in her mouth and crept up to the sleeping wolf and deposited them beside him. It was an impressive act of courage.

At daybreak Lamar woke with a start. When he spied the piece of meat beside him, I expected a rebuke for not waking him, but instead he cried:

"Oh, Maggie, this is the nicest gift I ever got!"

That day was even warmer. A couple of simpleminded nuthatches chirped over and over about the Merry Month of May. You could hear trickling under the snow. But there was no sign of Artemis.

Early the next morning Lamar went off to hunt. He tracked a fox down into what Frick had taught us was called a barranca—a sort of ravine—but when Lamar caught up to the fox it was already half eaten.

"Thought I got a whiff of you," Sully said, looking up from his meal. "Do you like fox?"

Lamar stared at his uncle in surprise. "I've never had any," he said.

"It's fairly disgusting but better than nothing. I'll leave the rest for you."

"Thank you, Uncle."

Sully studied him for a moment. "You know, Lamar," he said, "I like you. You're polite."

"Thank you," Lamar said again.

"What are you doing off on your own?"

I was curious to hear Lamar's answer. He hesitated a moment and said, "I'm taking a break from the pack."

"Are you?" Sully said. "That's brave. But life can be hard on your own, you know. Dangerous, too."

At a sudden noise both their heads spun around, but it was just a hunk of snow plopping off the tree I was in.

Sully licked a bit of fox fur off the tip of his snout. "Since you've left the pack, why don't you come along with me?"

"Where are you going?" said Lamar.

"Up north."

Lamar looked to the north—he'd clearly learned his

directions without the aid of a weather vane—but down in the barranca there wasn't much of a view. "What's up north?" he asked.

"The most delicious food in the world," Sully said. "Wait'll you taste it!"

"Elk?"

"Even better."

Lamar looked dubious.

"It's called cattle," Sully said.

"Never heard of it."

"They don't live in Yellowstone."

"What do they look like?"

"They're big. That's why I could use your help."

"As big as buffalo?"

"Almost."

"Did a cattle bite your ear off?"

"No, no."

"What's the cattle place called?"

"Montana."

"If Montana's so wonderful, why'd you come here?"

"Polite but full of questions," Sully murmured. "I came down here because I missed my brother. He's the only family I have. But the feeling doesn't seem to be mutual."

"I'm sorry for the way my father treated you," Lamar said gravely. "It wasn't right."

Sully shrugged and said, "Well, come to think of it, you're family too, aren't you? What do you say? Want to see the Big Sky Country?"

"The Big Sky Country?" Lamar said, his ears twitching with interest.

"Montana," I said. "But I wouldn't advise it. The ranchers there have guns, and they don't like wolves."

"How would you know?" Sully said.

"I was born and raised there."

Knowing Lamar, I figured the idea of a new place with novel creatures and a big sky would tempt him, so I was relieved when he heeded my advice and said, "Maybe another time." Though, of course, it may have been the idea of leaving Artemis's neighborhood that dissuaded him.

He and his uncle parted on good terms. Lamar took the remainder of the fox back to Artemis's cave and retreated to his usual spot. Day turned to night with no sign of her. To keep himself from falling asleep and missing her again, he recited some bird lore, mostly picked up from me.

"Bald eagles aren't really bald. Their heads are covered with snow-white feathers. Golden eagles are best avoided, but goldfinches are harmless. White pelicans have pouchy bills, though you don't want to get too close on account of their fish breath. Ravens are even blacker than Raze, and smarter, too, though not as smart as magpies or crows. Warblers have good voices, though Audubon says his high range was better when he was younger. Sapsuckers are showy but no brighter than nuthatches. Seagulls aren't particular. If there's no sea around, they'll use a lake. So will ruddy ducks and ospreys and scaups like Sabrina. Ospreys are excellent divebombers, but Peregrine falcons are faster. Mountain bluebirds are the color my eyes were when I was little. Now my eyes are more like a meadowlark."

He didn't mention swallows or owls, probably on account of the parts they'd played in Rider's death, and to be honest, I wouldn't have minded if he'd left out bluebirds. Once he got through all his birds, he started on lesser creatures. After that he listed the wonders he'd come across in Yellowstone, from geysers to mud volcanos. When he reached the end of his recitation, he started over.

By the third time through, we both started yawning.

I woke before him, at first light. Artemis had clearly come and eaten, for again there were leftovers not far from Lamar. They tempted me, but fond as I was of Lamar they were a little too close to his snout, so I flew off to the den site for a snack. The wolves were still in their energy-conserving mode, snoozing away, though I noticed they'd made quite a dent in the pile of buffalo meat. While I was taking a few pecks at it, Frick cracked an eye open.

"Blue Boy's been asking about Lamar," he said quietly. "Is he all right?"

I assured him that Lamar was fine.

Around midday I headed back to check on Lamar but got sidetracked when I spotted Sully. Despite the pretty picture he'd painted of Montana, he was heading west, not north. More surprising, he was on a hiking trail. The humans had made hundreds of miles of hiking trails in the huge park, and in a month or two they would be using them. But I'd never seen a wolf on one. Wolves like to blaze their own.

I alighted on a trail marker and introduced myself for the first time. Not even a mangy critter like Sully could resist chortling at my name.

"Guess the folks didn't put a lot of thought into it," he said.

"Well, my mother's Mag," I said, and switched the subject to Montana.

He must have been starved for company, for he chattered away, telling me all about how he'd ended up there.

After his release from the wolf compound years ago he'd joined a pack known as the Crystal Creek pack. He'd been at the bottom of their pecking order and got the poorest cuts of meat, but what really bugged him was being assigned to babysitting duty after the alpha pair whelped a litter of eight in the spring. The pups were relentless. Every time he was about to catch some sleep, one of them would jump on his back or nip his tail. He decided life on his own couldn't be worse than this, so he took off. But unlike the first time he dispersed, up in Canada, he didn't have Blue Boy with him. For a full year he skulked around Yellowstone as a lone wolf, barely surviving. Then he chased a deer into the Beartooth range, and through a cleft in the mountains he caught a glimpse of the ranching country to the north. Montana.

His first taste of livestock was sheep. It was tasty, though getting through all that wool was tedious. Cattle not only made an easier meal, but they were absolutely delicious. In no time he was hooked on beef. For over a year he lived in the foothills and made forays into the grazing land. But the rancher he was poaching from finally spotted him and got off a clear shot as the wolf cut across a snowy pasture. That was how Sully lost an ear. He couldn't even lick his wound, and having no one to nurse him made him bemoan his solitary state. So he ventured back down this way to try his luck with another pack. It was a surprise to come across one of Blue Boy's scent posts. He'd figured his brother had either gone back to Canada or died trying.

"I can't think why he was so ungracious," Sully told me.

I could, but I didn't mention that Blue Boy had confided in me. "Where are you heading now?" I asked.

He ducked his head and pawed his ear wound. "You seem like a solitary bird," he said. "Ever get sick of being on your own?"

This question ruffled my feathers. Didn't he realize I was part of his brother's pack? But then I guess it was an unusual situation. And did the wolves really feel that I was, now that I was of no use to them?

Sully went on without waiting for an answer. "Since Lamar doesn't want to go up to Montana, I'm sticking to my original plan. I heard there's a pack on the other side of Hellroaring Creek."

I followed him along the hiking trail till it led us into a grove of leafless cottonwood trees. First we heard Hellroaring Creek, then we saw it. It was so swollen and choc-a-bloc with tumbling chunks of ice that Sully decided it would be too much trouble to cross. Not far off was one of the log cabins human campers use in the summertime. Creeping under it, Sully spooked a hedgehog, but he let it waddle off, probably figuring a couple of mouthfuls weren't worth a snoutful of needles.

By then the sun was well off to the west, and I was about to go back to check on Lamar when wolves started howling across the river. Sully came out of his hiding place and howled back. The wolves gave him a cordial-sounding acknowledgment. Sully followed the hiking trail upstream and found a wooden bridge across the torrent. A scouting party of wolves met him on the other side: two males and a female. The female was about his size, the males a bit bigger, though neither looked like an alpha.

"I was wondering if I could join up with you," Sully said, his tail between his legs.

"You look a little the worse for wear," one of the males commented.

"It must be hard to hunt with only one ear," said the other.

"I got a fox just this morning," Sully said.

"Fox," the first male said contemptuously.

"Give me a chance," Sully said.

The three wolves exchanged glances. I must admit I

winced as Sully got down on his belly and groveled, his one ear flat against his skull.

"Well, pups are coming soon," the female said. "How do you feel about babysitting?"

"Oh," Sully cried, looking up happily. "I love pups!"

15

WHILE SULLY WAS INGRATIATING HIMSELF with this new pack, I heard the unmistakable roar of a mountain lion back to the east. I thought of Lamar, all on his own, and shot back in that direction.

It turned out Lamar wasn't in trouble. But his coyote friend was. A pair of the big cats had cornered Artemis in a box canyon on the east side of Druid Peak. I think I speak for all birds when I say cats are despicable, and mountain lions are the biggest ones in this part of the world. Like all cats, they enjoy nothing more than toying with their victims, and that's just what they were doing with poor Artemis, closing in on her little by little while she tried in vain to scale the canyon's sheer back wall.

I zoomed to the rocky knoll to alert Lamar. He wasn't there. I gave Slough Creek a fly-by, but Lamar hadn't rejoined the pack. He wasn't over by the hot springs, either.

Eventually I spotted him up on Specimen Ridge. I landed near him in a charred pine. But as I looked down at the handsome young wolf I realized I didn't want him torn limb from limb, and I decided to keep my mouth shut about Artemis. Against one mountain lion, he might have stood a chance, but not against two.

He didn't greet me very cheerfully.

"What's the matter?" I said.

"I can't find a thing for her, Maggie. There's so much melting snow—all the scents are washed away. I saw a bear. I think he'd just woken up from his winter nap. But I doubt Artemis likes bear."

"Mmm," I said, doubting Lamar could fell one.

He asked after the pack, and I told him that the buffalo meat and the warming weather were speeding his father's recovery remarkably.

"How's Hope?" he said.

"She seems back to a hundred percent. And she has Frick, of course. It's good to see Frick happy. And your mother's getting bigger and bigger. It won't be long."

"You haven't seen Artemis today, have you?"

I wished he hadn't asked that. "This tree suits me, don't you think?" I said evasively.

"How'd it get so black?"

"The wild fires of '88, I imagine. They're legendary. They say half the park went up in flames."

"You're kidding! Imagine if Artemis got caught in a fire! I'd kill myself."

I shot a guilty look toward Druid Peak. "You know, I might have seen a coyote," I said, figuring the miserable cats had probably finished their cruel work by now. "Over in that box canyon by Druid Peak."

"Was it Artemis?" he said eagerly.

"I'm not sure," I fudged. "But a couple of mountain lions seemed to have cornered—"

He was off before I could finish my sentence. I flapped after him, wondering if I should have kept my beak shut. If the mountain lions had made a meal of Artemis, Lamar would be inconsolable. If the merciless cats ate *him*, I would be.

When we got to the canyon, the cats were still at their sadistic business, poor Artemis still trying to claw her way up the cliff. Every time she tumbled back, shivering and soaked to the skin, into the wet snow at the foot.

Lamar had heard his father's call of the chase many times, but I'm pretty sure this was the first time he attempted one. Reverberating off the canyon walls, it sounded almost as deep and guttural as Blue Boy's. The mountain lions wheeled around in surprise. Lamar's neck arched. His ears, tail, and hackles shot straight up, and he snarled, narrowing his eyes to slits.

The surprise in the mountain lions' eyes quickly turned to menace. The smaller of the two probably outweighed Lamar by fifty pounds. As they started to move in on him, I squawked, "Run!" The obstinate young wolf held his ground, his tail flying high.

Then I heard a muffled drone.

Of all wingless species, human beings are the only ones who've managed to do something about their bird envy. They can actually get off the ground. But only in deafening, ungainly machines. I'd always considered these contraptions loathsome. Birds can get sucked into the engines and turned to mincemeat. But as one of these planes rumbled by overhead, probably on its way to the nearest airport, I was grateful for it. Like all cats, mountain lions are skittish beasts. One of the pair bounded away on Lamar's right, the other on his left. Lamar whirled around, but the cats had gone.

I was perched on some scree under the canyon's north wall. Now I flew over to a lichen-covered rock next to Lamar. He was panting as I'd never seen him, his sides heaving.

"It goes to show that humans aren't all bad," I said.

Once he caught his breath, he said:

"You're the one we should thank."

"We?" I said.

He turned to the back of the canyon. But there was no sign of Artemis. As soon as the plane had distracted her torturers, she'd fled for her life.

16

I FOLLOWED LAMAR BACK TO THE KNOLL in the waning daylight. I expected him to race to the top, but he curled up under a spruce near the bottom.

"Don't you want to see if Artemis is around?" I said.

"I can't go up there," he said. "I never found her any food."

Evidently he didn't think facing down two mountain lions on her behalf made up for this. I considered spending the night in the spruce, but Sully's comment about my being "solitary" gave me a hankering for the pack.

Though there were vestiges of the sunset in the

western sky when I landed in my aspen, the wolves had turned in. Blue Boy was sleeping by himself, which made me think Alberta had gone into the den to get ready to whelp her litter. Frick and Hope were curled up close by. Raze, Lupa, and Ben were farther up the slope. I wondered if any of them, even Blue Boy, had noticed that I'd been gone since midday. I was afraid they'd started thinking of me as little more than a scavenging hanger-on.

Despite all the flying I'd done that day, I was too fretful to sleep. And when I finally stuck my head under my wing, the sound of voices soon made me pull it back out. Raze and Lupa had come down the slope to talk in private. Their utter obliviousness to me didn't lift my spirits.

"Just yesterday you said you felt sorry for her for being so puffy and bloated," Raze said.

"But in a month she'll be coming out looking radiant," Lupa complained, "with a new litter in tow."

"Alberta could never look as good as you," Raze said.

"That may be, but I'm sick of her always taking precedence."

"Then let's do like we talked about. Ben's on board."

"If we leave to start a new pack, Blue Boy'll come after us and tear us to shreds."

"If he tries, I'll finish what that buffalo started."

"You really think you'd stand a chance, even with that wound of his?"

For a while there was only the burbling of the creek.

"We'll wait till the pups come out," Raze finally said. "He'll be in such a good mood, he won't care."

"He'll expect us to help feed them."

"Okay, when the pups join the hunt. Then he won't miss us."

"But you said this den site was your birthright. Where are we going to find such a perfect spot?"

If I hadn't been feeling sorry for myself, I might almost have felt sorry for Raze. For every answer he gave, Lupa had a retort.

They finally retreated up the slope to sleep, and I dozed off. In the morning I heard a magpie joining in with the thrushes and nuthatches across the creek to welcome the new day. Since coming to Yellowstone, I'd made a point of avoiding the local magpies, but I flew over now and struck up a conversation with this one, who was perched in a lodgepole pine. He was quite handsome, if a little young, and single. He even had a nest—an abandoned one he'd happened upon nearby.

"I don't suppose you'd like to see it?" he said.

"Why do you think that?"

"Birds say you're standoffish."

"That's ridiculous."

"Oh, good—I think you'll like it," he said eagerly. "I've done a lot of decorating."

"Decorating" should have set off warning bells, but I flew with him to see the nest. It was appalling. He was a worse trash collector than Dan. The floor was littered with bottle caps and paper clips and foil wrappers. On the walls were a rusted Smoky the Bear pin, an empty trail-mix bag, and a wilted 3-D postcard of Old Faithful. Like most magpie nests, his was hooded, and a laminated park-ranger badge hanging from the ceiling by a lanyard twisted slowly in the breeze.

"Isn't it great?" he cried. "All it needs is some eggs!"

"A pity I'm too old for that sort of thing," I said.

His face fell. It wasn't true, but I would have rather had my tail feathers plucked than be stuck egg sitting for weeks on end in that junkyard.

When I got back to my aspen, the wolves were up. The buffalo meat was almost gone, and Blue Boy, looking almost like his old self, ignored Frick's suggestion that he rest up another day. Hope went on the hunt too. I stayed behind with Frick, thinking that without Hope or Lamar he might appreciate my company. But he seemed content to sit watching the sun rise in the robin's egg blue sky.

When the hunters returned, Blue Boy set a piece of elk meat in the den entrance for Alberta and lay down to digest the meal he must have had at the kill site. I wanted to tell him what I'd overheard last night, but since he didn't so much as glance my way I kept my beak shut. I stayed in a sulky mood till late afternoon, when I flew over to the knoll. Lamar was in his usual spot. I asked after Artemis.

"Haven't seen her yet, but at least I got her something," Lamar said, nodding at an offering in the cave. "Thanks again for yesterday, Maggie. If those horrible cats had gotten her, I don't know what I would have done."

Sully was right about Lamar having good manners. For what are good manners, after all, but making others feel better? Grateful as I was to feel of *some* use, however, his focus understandably wasn't on me. I watched the top of the cliff along with him. The sun set, and a gibbous moon rose—and finally Artemis appeared. Her fur was a dusty gold in the moonlight, and her eyes, so panicked yesterday, sparkled playfully as she sniffed the air.

"It's mule deer," Lamar told her. "I got him by Soda Butte."

"I never tried mule deer," she said.

"It's a thigh. I hope you like it."

"Would you mind . . . ?"

Lamar trotted away. Once he was on the far side of a gulch, Artemis circled down off the cliff and sampled the deer. By bird standards her table manners were crude, but compared to wolves, she ate primly. When she finished, she hiked back up to her perch, and Lamar returned to his previous spot.

"What do you think?" he said.

"Well, it's filling," she said. "Oh, wow! Did you catch it?"

"By Soda Butte, like I said."

"I meant that shooting star."

I searched the night sky along with him. "Darn," he said.

"It was a beauty," Artemis said. "Oh, and you won't believe what I saw this afternoon."

"What?" Lamar said.

"An osprey dropped a fish, and a bear grabbed it in midair."

"I thought osprey never dropped fish."

"They never do. It was unique."

Lamar turned my way and said in an undertone: "What's 'unique'?"

"Something that happens only once," I said.

Artemis added something, but too softly to make out.

"Excuse me, Artemis?" Lamar said.

"I said, 'Like a wolf saving a coyote from mountain lions.'"

"Oh, but I'd do the same thing if it happened again."

"Well, let's hope it remains unique."

With that, Artemis disappeared.

"I don't think 'filling' means she liked the mule deer much," Lamar said with a sigh.

"I've heard more ringing endorsements," I said.

"Vole's her favorite. I'll try to catch her one tomorrow."

I didn't find out if he succeeded. Though Lamar made me feel welcome, I sensed that three was a crowd on the knoll.

I returned to my usual routine, hanging out in my aspen and accompanying the pack on the hunt. It should have been a joyful time. Herds of elk and pronghorn had migrated back up into the valley, which was turning greener by the day. And a few days later the sound of newborns could be heard from the den: at least four different yaps. But with no Lamar around, and Frick so content, and Blue Boy so focused on the den, I felt more useless than ever.

One morning Blue Boy got up with the sun and padded down the hill. I figured he wanted a drink from the creek, but he stopped under my aspen and looked up at me.

"Have you seen him?" he asked.

"Who?" I said—though of course I knew.

"Lamar."

"Not lately."

"He just took off—not even a good-bye. Wolves don't usually disperse till after they're two, you know. Why do you think he did?"

"You don't have any ideas?"

Blue Boy sniffed. "He did question the way I treated my brother . . ."

"Don't forget how devastated he was when we lost Rider. He's a sensitive wolf."

"Sensitive wolf," Blue Boy said, spitting out the words. But then he sighed. "If he'd just taken off like a normal hotheaded kid instead of sticking around to make sure . . ."

"You had that buffalo to tide you over," I said, finishing his thought. "Do you miss him?"

Blue Boy didn't reply.

"There's nothing wrong with missing him," I said. "He is your son."

"Where'd he go, Maggie?"

"Why ask me?"

"You think I didn't notice how you stayed home from the hunt the same days he did?"

I admit it was good to hear he paid attention to my movements. "I may have seen him a while back."

"Where?" he pressed.

"You can't tell him I told you."

"I won't."

I pointed my beak to the southeast. "There's a rocky knoll down that away."

He nodded. "Thanks."

"And Blue Boy?"

"Hmm?"

"There's something you might be interested to know about Raze and Lupa."

"That they're planning to go off and start their own pack with Ben?"

"How'd you know?" I said, stupefied.

"I may not have a bird's-eye view of things, but I have eyes and ears. Coming on the hunt today?"

Brooding can make you lose weight, and when you start at half a pound, you can't afford to lose much. So I went. With Blue Boy and Hope both on the road to full recovery, the pack made short work of a tawny elk cow who'd strayed from her herd. After filling his belly, Blue Boy tore off a nice portion for Alberta and her brood, but the rest of us remained at the kill site and stuffed ourselves. I woke shamefully late the next morning. The wolves were even more lethargic, except for Blue Boy. He was gone—on an expedition to the southeast, I suspected.

Blue Boy got back before the other wolves stirred, and he parked himself under my aspen, which was now stippled with tight red buds.

"You were right about that knoll," he said. "When you see him from below, you realize how big he's gotten."

"Almost as big as you. Did you talk?"

"No. There was a coyote on the summit. I figured he was stalking her, so I kept quiet. But when I crept a little closer I realized he wasn't stalking—he was talking! To a coyote! She didn't look the least bit worried. Relaxed muzzle, ears back. Seemed interested in what he was saying."

In all the time I'd known Blue Boy, I'd never heard him string so many words together. "What was he saying?" I asked.

"Don't know and don't care. It's got to stop. No future in it. He's got my blood. He can't pass it on with a coyote."

"You just left?"

"I felt like grabbing him by the scruff of the neck

and dragging him back. But he's stubborn. He'd just leave again. We have to get him to come back on his own."

"How do you plan to do that?" I asked.

"Do you think you could find my brother? Tell him I was in a rotten mood that day?"

"You mean you'd let him into the pack?"

"Then if Lamar hears about it, it might bring him back and save him from this lunacy. Think you could find Sully?"

"He may have joined another pack, but I can try."

I must admit it felt good to be needed. I set off to the west before the other wolves had woken from their stupor-ish sleep. On the other side of Hellroaring Creek I ran into a hunting party that included the three wolves who'd taken Sully into their pack. I asked them if Sully was at their den site.

"One Ear?" said the female. "He took off the other day."

I asked why, and she admitted they'd given him a rough time—calling him names and treating him like a court jester and leaving him only the gristliest bits of meat.

"Something tells me he wasn't really looking forward to babysitting, either," she said. "He didn't even wait to see the pups."

"Do you know which way he went?"

"North."

I could just picture it. Stuck with crummy scraps, Sully had probably gone to sleep with visions of succulent cuts of beef dancing in his head. I would have bet my beak he'd headed back to Montana.

In my gloom I'd actually contemplated going back there myself—and now I was. Spring was a nice time for it. When I soared over the Beartooth Mountains, the grazing land that stretched out before me was a tender green, the rivers full to the brim, the hillsides speckled with wild flowers. I was looking for Sully, but I couldn't resist flying up to the Triple Bar T and spending the night in my old ponderosa pine, with its cozy vanilla smell. There was no sign of the cluttered nest or of Dan. He must have died or been killed, for I couldn't imagine him moving away. First thing in the morning I flew down to the base of the big cottonwood. At first I was sorry that someone had filled in the hole between the roots; then I realized I wouldn't really have wanted to confront Jackson's skeleton. I flew up to his old perch on the weather vane. A magpie doing figure eights around the silos might have been my sister Marge. I also spotted a couple of my kids: Denny or Danny, I wasn't quite sure, and Anastasia. But they were busy with their nesting, and if they recognized me, they didn't acknowledge me. Of course, they'd hardly seen me since they were fledglings. I hadn't been much of a mother.

Before long the screen door slammed and out of the house sauntered Red Cap. He was as tall as his father now, and the cap had faded to a dirty rose. He still had a rifle, though. And there was still a ragged silhouette of a wolf on the target. When he took a shot at it, my heart lurched in my chest. I'd been away from my wolves less than two days, but even though I doubted they missed me, I missed them.

I remembered I was on a mission and flew back to the south. When I reached the last ranch before the foot-hills, I landed atop a windmill. It was a big spread, and I figured it was probably the one Sully raided for cattle. But although there were plenty of steers, and cowboys on horseback with dogs trailing along behind, there was no sign of any wolf.

I settled in for the night, thinking Sully might do his marauding under the cover of darkness. The moon was dull, with a halo around it, but it showed up a glint of eyes near the barn. I flew down for a closer look. It was just a housecat slinking around after mice or rats.

In the morning I made another tour of the place. The rancher came out of the house and climbed into a pickup.

He started to drive away but stopped by a corral full of horses to talk to a cowhand sitting on the fence. I landed on the fence in time to hear the rancher say something about a wolf.

"Same dang critter, I'm sure of it," he said.

"Blue one?" asked the cowboy.

"Yup. I called those dang tree huggers down in Yellowstone."

"Are they gonna get off their butts this time?"

"They already knew he'd come back up here. Tracking doohickey in the collar. They said he's headed back to them now."

"Like I said, sir," the cowhand said, spitting a stream of brown juice onto the ground, "are they gonna get off their butts this time?"

Across the corral a horse whinnied. A closer horse flapped his gums, and I missed the rancher's reply. Once the horses settled down, I heard the rancher say:

"May not need to, though. Think I winged him."

With that he drove away, kicking up so much dust, I had to fly straight up into the air to keep from choking. Wolves are as wingless as humans, and as I flapped off to the south, I wondered what "winged him" meant. I had an idea what "doohickey" meant. The collars on the original wolves from Canada must have had tracking devices in them. Blue Boy had played a good trick on the humans by getting his shot off.

Halos around the moon usually mean a coming storm, and as I flew into the foothills, the clouds thickened and, even though it was mid-May, the temperatures dropped sharply. When the snow began to fall, I took shelter in a hemlock tree.

That night the storm dumped over a foot. But by daybreak it had passed, and the pristine world it left behind was a joy to fly over. What's more, without the new snow I never would have found Sully. As I was passing through a notch between two peaks, I spotted a strand of red drops on the blanket of white. At the end of the trail of blood Sully was curled up at the foot of a snowdrift.

His spirits were very low. By "winged him" the rancher must have meant "shot him," for there was now a bullet hole in his left rear thigh to go along with his missing ear.

"You know the name of that mountain over there?" he said, pointing his snout.

"No," I said.

"Froze-to-Death Mountain. Appropriate, don't you think?"

"You're not going to freeze to death."

"Why not? Not much point in going on. Nobody gives a hoot about me."

"Blue Boy does."

Sully snorted, his breath vaporizing in the cold, dry air.

"He wants you in his pack," I said.

"Yeah, right."

"Why do you think I'm here? He sent me specially to look for you."

A glimmer of hope crept into Sully's eyes. He was in pretty bad shape, but hope is the best medicine in the world, and he made it through the snowy mountain pass and back down onto what's called Buffalo Plateau, on the northern border of Yellowstone. What snow had fallen there melted in the course of that day. At nightfall we collapsed by a pond. In the morning we found that it was a beaver pond, but different from Sabrina's, far bigger, with dead, half-submerged trees poking spookily out of the boggy water. Sully crept along the bank, his eyes fixed on a wake moving across on the pond's surface. It was too small to be a beaver's, and when Sully jumped in after it, I caught sight of a muskrat darting off into a hole in the bank. But in spite of his wound, Sully didn't give up. Instead of climbing out, he stood knee-deep in the pond, his eyes fixed on something else in the water. He took a step, froze, took another step, and froze again. Finally he threw himself into a little inlet and, to my astonishment, came up with a fish in his mouth. I'd never heard of a wolf fishing. Maybe he'd picked up the skill during his long, first year as a lone wolf. But it was a small fish, and I doubt the energy he'd expended was worth the morsel. He climbed out of the water and trudged past the beaver lodge and dam, still looking around hungrily. His head hung lower and lower as we followed Buffalo Creek downstream to where it merged with Slough Creek.

When we came around the boulder below the den site, Blue Boy and the rest of the pack were lounging outside the whelping den. I couldn't tell if they'd gone hunting that morning or not, though there was some fresh-looking meat on an elk bone Blue Boy was gnawing. I landed in my aspen. Just since I'd been gone, leaves had broken out of their buds, like butterflies out of their cocoons. Sully stayed down by the stream, his tail between his legs, studying the muddy ground.

Blue Boy rose to his feet, gave me a nod of acknowledgement, and fixed his gaze on his brother. "It's good to see you, Sully," he said.

Sully lifted his eyes. I don't think I've ever seen anyone look so grateful.

"Join us," Blue Boy said.

"That doesn't look so good, Uncle," Hope said, noticing Sully's latest wound as he came up the slope.

"Maybe I can help," Frick said, and he trotted off into the woods.

"Was it an antler?" Hope wondered.

"Something like that," Sully said, settling near her. "Looks like you had a little run-in yourself."

"Only a branch," Hope said sheepishly. "It's pretty much healed."

Sully gave his brother a timid look. "I heard you tangled with a buffalo, Blue Boy."

"Just a scratch," Blue Boy said, shoving the bone his way.

Frick returned with some healing herbs and laid them by the bone. But famished as he was, Sully was too dazed by his good fortune to touch either. His ear twitched as yapping came from inside the den.

"A new litter?" he asked.

"Five, I think," Blue Boy said proudly.

"How wonderful!" Sully cried. "I love pups!"

17

THE NEXT MORNING SULLY MADE A FEEBLE OFFER to join the hunting party, but in his current condition he would have been more hindrance than help, and he put up no argument when Blue Boy told him to stay home and let Frick tend to him. Blue Boy led the rest of us along the ridge trail. It was quite a warm day, but as soon as we got down into the valley I heard what sounded like a branch snapping in the cold.

Blue Boy slumped to the ground. When I realized he'd been shot, my wings faltered and I lost altitude. Barely catching myself, I swooped over to him. Hope rushed up and, crouching at his side, started licking at something stuck in his flank. Blue Boy lifted his head, panting furiously. In a moment his head fell back onto the grass, and his panting stopped.

Raze, Lupa, and Ben were watching from a ways off, but a mechanical noise soon sent them skedaddling. Hope remained at Blue Boy's side till a vehicle came jouncing right up to us. It was the same four-wheeler I'd seen at the wolf compound, and the two humans who climbed out of it were the same ones I'd seen there as well. They approached Blue Boy cautiously. The male with the furry face carried a rifle, the female with the long wheaten hair, a blanket. Furry Face poked Blue Boy with the rifle barrel. Blue Boy didn't as much as twitch. The humans wrapped him in the blanket and loaded him into the back of the four-wheeler.

I never thought I'd feel more devastated than when Trilby said, "Maggie, what on earth are you doing here?" I was wrong. But, unlike then, I wasn't paralyzed. The only way I would have let Blue Boy's body out of my sight was if the humans had shot me, too.

I tore after the four-wheeler and followed it out of the valley and over three or four ridges to the compound. The humans parked outside the A-frame and carried Blue Boy's blanket-wrapped body into the garage. There was a cage in there that hardly looked big enough to hold him, but they shoved him in it anyway. Horrible as this was, I figured it was better than a hole in the ground.

As on my first visit, one of the outdoor pens was occupied: this time by a snow-white female wolf with a splint on her left hind leg. I landed on the chain-link fence, and as soon as the humans disappeared into the A-frame, I squawked:

"He was just going hunting and the humans shot him!"

"You're kidding!" the she-wolf said. "They saved me."

"Saved you?"

"A semi hit me on the interstate. The humans found me half-dead on the side of the road and brought me here. Ah, I thought so—look."

There was movement in the shadowy cage. Blue Boy was shedding the blanket and struggling to his feet! I dislike enclosed spaces, but I swooped into the garage and landed on the cage.

"Maggie," he said, looking at me groggily.

"Are you okay?"

He didn't answer.

"What's that thing in your side?" I said.

Only noticing it now, he worried it with his teeth till it

fell onto the bottom of the cage: a tiny tube with a needle at one end and what looked ominously like a tiny bird feather on the other. I hopped down onto a latch on the side of the cage and pecked it so hard my bill almost cracked.

It still hadn't opened when I heard the squeak of a screen door. As the two human beings walked into the garage, I shot out onto the four-wheeler's tailgate. The humans went up to the cage and peered in.

"He already got the dart out," said Furry Face.

Blue Boy lunged at them, smacking his snout against the bars. The humans jumped back.

"What a beast!" Furry Face said. "I shouldn't have let you talk me out of killing him."

"He's magnificent," said Golden Hair.

"He is something, but he has to be destroyed," Furry Face said. "What's the point of prolonging it? If we let him go and he heads north again, that rancher could get our funding cut off."

"We agreed we have to be sure it's the right wolf. The rancher said he just shot him. That wound's not fresh."

"He said the wolf was blue. And his tracker put him at Slough Creek."

"But we brought down *two* blue ones from British Columbia. Remember the big one that dug his way out?"

"He got killed up on the Montana-Idaho border."

"That's what we decided because—wait, Brian, look! He has no collar."

"Good grief. You're right."

"Check the tracker."

I stayed put as Furry Face passed by me on his way out of the garage. He ducked into one of the trailers. Soon he came hurrying back.

"Unbelievable," he said. "There are still four by Slough Creek."

"We've got the wrong blue wolf," said Golden Hair. "Aren't you glad we used the tranquilizer?"

If the only wolves they'd put tracking collars on were the original ones from Canada, the four had to be Alberta, Frick, Lupa, and Sully. They must have been able to follow Sully's trek to and from Montana. But while they realized they'd tranquilized Blue Boy by mistake they decided not to set him free, reasoning that if there were *two* bluish wolves out there it would make sense to keep this one locked up till they got the cattle killer, to prevent another mix-up.

"Want to move him to one of the pens?" Golden Hair said.

"It'll be a lot easier to leave him in the cage," said Furry Face. "I can drive him back over there and release him after I track down the culprit—first thing tomorrow. Live ammo this time. There can't be *three* blue wolves."

"I'll grind up some of that sedative in this guy's food to calm him down."

Furry Face went off into the A-frame, Golden Hair into another of the trailers. Golden Hair soon came back with a bowl of some kind of chopped meat and slid it through a flap under the door of Blue Boy's cage. She flicked on a garage light before pulling the door down behind her.

I wished she'd left the door open. Now I couldn't clue Blue Boy in on the humans' conversation, which I knew he hadn't understood. And though the door had a window in the top panel, I wasn't a hummingbird and couldn't hover outside looking in. The best I could do was hop up onto the four-wheeler's roll bar and watch over him through the pane of dirty glass. He gave the bowl of food a contemptuous sniff but didn't eat any. And though he barely had room to turn around in the cage, he kept twisting this way and that. As the daylight waned, he got more and more agitated. I knew he was thinking about the den full of newborns he was responsible for feeding. The darker it grew outside, the more vividly I could see him in the lit-up garage. One of his deep-throated howls might have attracted the humans' attention, but he didn't howl—he just kept squirming around. Then he pressed himself against the back of the cage and launched a vicious attack on the bars. It was a gruesome spectacle, and I wanted to look away, like when he'd fought Raze's father. But I couldn't. I squawked for Blue Boy to quit. He kept at it in a blind fury. Then I thought I saw a tooth fly out of his mouth, and in my horror, I threw myself right into the window. But whether or not this distracted him from his self-destruction, I couldn't say, for I fell to the ground in a daze.

18

THE SQUEAK OF A SCREEN DOOR brought me around. It was early morning, and Golden Hair was coming out of the A-frame. Righting myself on the hard-packed dirt, I shook the dust off my feathers and scuttled out of her way as she approached the garage. When she lifted the garage door, she let out a gasp.

"Brian!" she yelled. "The wolf—I think he's dead!"

I made a clumsy takeoff and managed to swerve by her and make a pass over the cage. I caught only a glimpse of Blue Boy, but it was enough. He was lying in a crimson pool, his beautiful blue coat smeared with blood and bits of chopped meat. Near the tipped-over bowl lay one of the glorious incisors he used for ripping out elks' wind-pipes. In a moment, Furry Face came running into the garage, and I flapped awkwardly away.

As I flew out of the compound, I knew I should go back to the den site to tell the others the dreadful news, but I had to land in a lodgepole pine and collect myself. I was having trouble breathing. I couldn't believe that magnificent wolf who could shoot through forests and bring down creatures three times his size would never move again. It seemed so terribly wrong, a crime against nature.

When the sun rose over the treetops, I set out for Slough Creek. I couldn't fly quite straight, so I aimed a little left of where I wanted to go.

Once I got to my aspen, I saw that Raze, Lupa, and Ben were up near the top of the hill with their heads together. I couldn't hear what they were talking about, but I could hear the whine of pups from inside the den, and Frick and Hope conversing in low tones near the entrance.

"I shouldn't have told her," Frick was saying.

"It's throwing her nursing off, no doubt about it," Hope said. "But you couldn't keep it from her."

It sounded as if they'd told Alberta, who must have still been in the den, that Blue Boy had been killed. So at least I was spared having to break the unspeakable news.

"I always thought he was invincible," Frick said. "Utterly invincible."

"It doesn't seem real," Hope said bleakly. "Do you suppose Uncle Sully's right, that they were actually after *him*?"

"It would be quite a coincidence otherwise, him showing up and Blue Boy getting shot the very next day. I heard him slink off in the night."

"He must feel awfully guilty. I wonder where he went."

So did I. I cared about a tenth as much about Sully as I did his brother, but it didn't seem right not to warn him that Furry Face could track him by his collar and was coming after him with real bullets. I was so cast down that I hadn't even noticed what a glorious spring day it was, but as I flew a little crookedly out over the valley it was impossible not to. The river, surging with snowmelt, was almost as blue as Trilby. The trees on the banks were dusted a green so pale it was almost yellow, and the antlers of the young bucks were sheathed in ruddy velvet. I found Sabrina and Audubon chatting by the bank of the pond. Sabrina hadn't noticed any wolves that day, but Audubon had seen one heading toward Buffalo Creek.

"Did he have a bluish tinge to his coat?" I asked.

"Sorry, didn't notice," Audubon said. "All wolves look the same to me."

I hadn't seen Sabrina since fall, so she had to tell me about her winter down south before I could head off toward Buffalo Creek. On this side of the woods that hid the creek I spotted a wolf moving through the tall grass. From a distance only his tail and the top of his head were visible, but I could tell it wasn't Sully, for the wolf had both his ears. As I got closer, I saw it was Lamar. From the spring in his step I knew he hadn't heard about the shooting.

"Hi, Maggie!" he said as I landed nearby. "Have you seen any voles?"

"Sorry, no," I said.

"I saw a shrew, and a garter snake, but I wanted to get Artemis her favorite today. Last night we talked for hours!"

I wasn't sure I wanted to be the one to tell him that while he'd been enjoying his coyote friend's company, his father had been killing himself against the steel bars of a cage.

Lamar trotted on into the woods, found the creek, and had a good slurp. I took a little drink myself and then fluttered up into one of the cottonwoods. With his thirst quenched Lamar sniffed at a cluster of tiny purple flowers by his feet. Suddenly his ears flattened, pressing outward, and his muzzle twitched. Across the creek a grouse burst out of a bush and shot up through the budding trees.

A one-eared wolf came slinking along the opposite bank, his head low to the ground, his feet making squishing sounds in the wet mat of last year's leaves.

"Hello, Uncle," Lamar said.

"Lamar!" Sully exclaimed. "What are you doing here?"

"Hunting voles."

"You like *vole*?"

"It's for a friend."

Sully cast a glance over his shoulder, then gave Lamar a baleful look. "I'm sorry about your father," he said.

Lamar stiffened. "My father? What about him?"

"You don't know? He got shot."

"What?"

"Yesterday, on his way to the hunt."

"He's not . . . dead?"

Sully hesitated. "I hate to carry bad news, but that's what Hope told us. She said the humans collected the carcass."

Lamar looked thunderstruck. There was no point in telling them that Blue Boy hadn't been a carcass yet when the humans had collected him. For a long time the two wolves just stood with the water sluicing between them.

"What a wolf he was," Sully said mournfully.

It seemed to take a while for Lamar to register his uncle's words. A flicker of surprise crossed his face. "You're sorry he's gone after the way he treated you?" he said.

"You mean sending me packing that time?" Sully sniffed. "I deserved it. He never told you how we parted years ago?"

Lamar shook his head. Sully told him how he'd helped dig the tunnel out of the pen in the compound and then refused to use it.

"Blue Boy needed my help to protect his family back up in Canada. But it was so cushy there, I wouldn't go. I'll remember the look he gave me till the day I die. I was always a lot smaller than him, but that morning I felt like a mouse. He never told you about the owl, either?"

Lamar blinked at him. "The one that got Rider?"

"Who's Rider?"

"My little brother."

"I don't know about that. But when I was a pup, an owl grabbed me. I was heading up into the sky when Blue Boy made an amazing leap and clamped onto my hind leg. The weight of two pups was too much for the nasty bird, and he let us go."

Lamar's jaw went slack. No doubt he was thinking

he might have done the same for Rider. I thought back to that day, too, realizing now why Blue Boy had been so sure in identifying the owl.

"I never properly appreciated my brother," Sully said. "But a couple of days ago he took me into his pack anyway."

"He did?" Lamar said, stunned.

"Yes. And see how I repaid him."

Lamar stared at him.

"The humans were after me, not him," Sully explained. "I'm sure of it. I might as well have pulled the trigger myself."

Lamar said nothing, but I had an idea what he was feeling. He'd left the pack because of his father treating his brother poorly, and now that very brother was singing Blue Boy's praises—eulogizing him. It's always disturbing to learn you've gotten things wrong, but gut-wrenching when it's too late to do anything about it.

"I'm sorry I ever came back down here," Sully said, turning away.

"Where are you going?" I asked.

Sully glanced back, giving a loose shrug. "I don't know. Who cares?"

This seemed to penetrate Lamar's despondency. "Are

you going back to where those cattle live?" he asked.

Sully shrugged again and gave the wound on his thigh a lick.

"You can come with me if you want," Lamar said.

Sully looked at his nephew, his eyes softening for a moment. "I appreciate that, Lamar. But I'm afraid I have to say the same thing to you I once said to your father."

A breeze rustled through the trees.

"What's that smell?" Lamar said, sniffing.

I thought I caught a whiff of human. However, Sully didn't seem to, for he started talking about the last time he and Lamar had met. "Remember where it was?" he asked.

"The barranca near the knoll," Lamar said. "You'd caught a fox."

"That's right. I passed through there this morning and saw some voles."

"I looked there already."

"Down in the very bottom. A regular convention of them. If I were you, I'd get a move on before it breaks up."

I think Lamar was in such a state of heartbroken guilt over his father that for a moment not even the prospect of getting Artemis her favorite food could shake it. But before long, Sully's words sank in, and Lamar tore off through the woods.

"It's funny, that kid almost makes me wish I'd had pups of my own," Sully said, watching him go.

I got another whiff of human. Soon I spotted Furry Face approaching stealthily through the trees.

"You better move it too," I said. "The human's using real bullets."

"To tell you the truth, bird, I'm sick of moving," Sully said. "What I'd like is a nice, long sleep."

Sully took a drink from the creek. When he lifted his head, water drooled off his snout and whiskers. Then there was a sharp crack, and my tree shivered. At the next crack Sully twisted around, crabbed sideways a few steps, and sank to the ground.

Furry Face tromped out of the trees. He was carrying a rifle, the barrel lowered. He came up and stood over the fallen wolf. When he nudged him with a boot, Sully didn't stir. The man squatted down to examine Sully's bullet wounds—one brand new, one a few days old—then stood up again.

"I'm sorry, fella, but I had no choice," Furry Face said sadly. "Why'd you have to go killing cattle?"

I stayed in my cottonwood as Furry Face trudged off downstream. A dark splotch was spreading in the fur at Sully's neck.

"I guess you were about ready, old wolf," I said quietly.

It startled me when one of his eyes opened.

"I thought you were gone," I said.

"Playing possum," he said.

"Can you get up?"

Sully tried but didn't make it to his feet. I caught a glint of panic in his eyes.

"Don't leave me?" he said.

"I won't," I said, and I flitted over to a tree on his side of the creek.

He drifted in and out of consciousness all that afternoon as the bloodstain darkened his whole neck. At dusk, clouds blew in, making for a starless, moonless night. I could barely make out the dying wolf below me. Every now and then I heard a raspy breath over the sound of running water. But few things induce sleep like a murmuring creek, and I finally dozed off.

A ragged cry woke me with a start. A faint light was filtering in through the prison bars of the trees. I looked down and met a pair of yellow, terror-stricken eyes. The blood had soaked Sully's whole chest, merging with the dried blood from his older wound. I dropped down and landed not far from his head. I suspected that the "vole convention" had just been a way of getting Lamar out of harm's way, and I thanked Sully for looking out for his nephew.

"You were a good uncle to him," I said.

Sully stared at me a moment, then laid his head down on the moldering leaves and closed his eyes. His chest rose and fell for a while, but slower and slower, till at last he was still.

19

IT WASN'T AS BAD AS WITH JACKSON'S CORPSE. I hadn't known or loved Sully nearly as well, plus I was older now and knew how littered life is with death. But even if Sully had been lazy and spineless he'd muddled along by his own dim lights, and now they'd gone out forever. It's awful to look at someone who can no longer look back at you, who will never look back at anyone. Though at the same time, to be honest, you do feel a flicker of gratitude that it's not you.

The clouds were still thick, but more daylight was leaking into the woods, and a few thrushes and vireos began to sing, in their tuneless way. Even now it seemed heartless to desert Sully. But all at once the singing stopped. A pair of enormous buzzards flapped down through the treetops. I shot off into a tree across the creek as they landed on either side of Sully's body. It didn't take them long to start doing what buzzards do. I couldn't stop them, and it was too painful to watch, so I flapped away.

As I passed over the ridge trail—I was flying straighter now—I spotted Hope, dropped down, and landed on a toadstool just off the trail.

"What are you doing out here by yourself?" I said.

"Somebody has to get food for Alberta and the babies," she said.

"What about Raze and Lupa and Ben?"

"I'd like to tell you they're in mourning." She sniffed. "But if you ask me, they're plotting something."

"You shouldn't hunt alone, Hope."

She was small and delicate—for a wolf—and it wasn't so long ago that she'd been speared by that branch. But she shrugged her narrow shoulders and moved determinedly on down the trail. I fluttered after her. From the promontory a big herd of elk could be seen on this side of the river. A bull and a cow and two calves had strayed from the crowd. But instead of waiting in the tall grass till one of the calves wandered away from his mother, Hope went after the bull. I couldn't squawk at her without spooking her prey. She crept upwind of him almost as silently as her father would have done. The bull's uneven gait made me think he was slightly addled—he'd probably gotten his skull cracked fighting over the cow in rutting season—but this didn't make Hope's targeting him any less distressing. When Hope leaped onto the bull's shoulder, he tried to gouge her with his antlers. She clung to him tenaciously. He finally managed to knock her off, only to have her jump right back on and sink her fangs into him again. The bull writhed and thrashed but finally stumbled. Once he was on his knees, Hope went straight for his windpipe.

By the end Hope was exhausted. And after all that effort she didn't take a single bite, simply stripping off a big hunk of the haunch and lugging it back up onto the ridge trail.

When we reached the den site, Frick was drinking from the creek. The other three wolves were uphill from the den, Raze sharing a bone with Ben while Lupa groomed herself.

"Why didn't you wake me?" Frick called out as Hope dropped the meat by the den entrance. "You shouldn't go hunting by yourself."

Before Hope could even answer, Raze had hustled down to her. "What do you think you're doing?" he said, eyes narrowed.

"Getting Mother food so she can nurse—what does it look like?" Hope said.

"You should offer me the first taste."

Hope snorted contemptuously. Raze shot forward, grabbed her by the neck, and tossed her down the hill toward my aspen. I squawked in outrage. Not only did Raze have a size advantage, but Hope had expended every ounce of her energy bringing down that elk. While my squawk still hung in the air, Frick sprinted up the hill and attacked Raze. Raze spun away and raked Frick's scarred backside with his claws. Frick yelped and scrambled back to where Hope lay panting.

"Bring it to me," Raze said, his voice laced with threat.

By now Lupa and Ben were standing behind him. Hope struggled to her feet, but neither she nor Frick made a move toward the den, so Ben grabbed the piece of elk and dragged it to Raze. Raze tore off about a third and started chomping.

"That's meant for Alberta," Frick said, blood streaming down his furless hind legs.

Raze dropped the meat and gave Frick a look of cold

menace. "The first taste goes to the alpha," he said.

"And you think that's you?"

"I suppose *you* are?" Lupa said, nostrils flaring.

"Alberta's our leader now," Frick said.

"She's suckling pups," Lupa said.

"I hunted that for them," Hope said angrily.

"Tell you the truth, I'm not so sure I want a bunch of Blue Boy's pups around," Raze said. "Next year Lupa and I'll make our own."

"You'd let the pups starve?" Frick said incredulously. "Are you out of your mind?"

Raze was on him in a flash, this time clamping his jaws around Frick's throat. Hope threw herself on Raze, but Lupa and Ben yanked her off. Forcing Frick to the ground, Raze snarled the bloodcurdling snarl of the kill.

I flew up in the air and was about to dive-bomb him when I saw a wolf come over the crest of the hill. A big wolf. At first I doubted my eyes. I flew up to the top of the hill and saw that the wolf's coat, though spattered with dirt and dried blood, had patches of blue showing through. I zipped back to my aspen and crowed.

"Father!" Hope cried.

Raze let go of Frick and jumped backward. Hope threw herself over Frick like a shield. Lupa's ears shot back, pinned against her head. So did Ben's.

Then another astounding thing happened. Alberta never deserted her suckling newborns, but suddenly there she was, bounding out of the den. She whirled around and cried:

"Blue Boy!"

Hearing Alberta say his name dispelled any lingering doubts I may have had. Blue Boy truly was here. He was wagging his tail at the sight of his mate.

"Are the pups all right?" he said.

"Didn't you get shot?" Alberta cried.

"Yes. Are the pups all right?"

"They're fine!"

"And you, Frick?" Blue Boy asked.

Frick just lay there.

"Raze was trying to kill him, Father," Hope said.

"Why would you do that, Raze?" Blue Boy said, his eyes slits.

For a moment Raze looked as if he'd turned to stone. Then he shrugged and said, "We were just sparring."

"Liar," Hope hissed. "You were trying to take over the pack."

"We thought you were dead," Raze said, his eyes fixed on Blue Boy.

"That much is true," Alberta said, ignoring whines from the den. "I haven't slept for two nights. Where have you been?"

"The place the humans first brought us," Blue Boy said.

"You're not hurt?"

Instead of answering, he walked down and gave her a nuzzle. "I think they used the same kind of bullet as up in Canada," he said.

Frick groaned.

"Have some elk, Blue Boy," Lupa said.

Blue Boy picked up the larger of the two chunks of meat, but instead of eating it he tossed it gingerly into the den.

"Better get back to the pups, Alberta," he said.

Alberta gave him a tender look and followed the food inside. I don't think she noticed the blood trickling down the side of his muzzle. But by the way Raze's ears pricked up, I was pretty sure *he* did.

20

I KNEW WHAT A MESS BLUE BOY'S MOUTH MUST be—I'd witnessed the attack on the unforgiving steel bars that had left the broken-off tooth lying in the pool of his own blood. It was incredible that he wasn't dead. I'd seen humans do wonders with lame horses and sick cattle up on the Triple Bar T, but Golden Hair must have performed a miracle on Blue Boy while Furry Face was out stalking Sully.

Curious as I was about it, I figured what Blue Boy needed now wasn't questions but backup. I flew straight— or almost straight—to the rocky knoll. Lamar was curled up asleep near the foot of the knoll, where he slept when he hadn't gotten Artemis any food. I landed in a twisted cedar and squawked:

"Come with me!"

Lamar sat up and yawned, displaying his impressive teeth.

"Your father needs you, Lamar," I said.

Lamar's face turned grim. "My father's dead."

"No, he's not. He's at the den site. But he's in troub—"

Lamar was off before I could finish. He sprinted across the flatland, his big feet sending up sprays of moisture from the newly thawed ground. When he reached Slough Creek, it was looking more like Slough River, but he splashed his way up the flooded bank, not stopping till he reached the boulder.

I doubt the other wolves noticed me returning to my aspen. Blue Boy was standing on one side of the den, his whole body tensed and his tail straight up. On the other side stood Raze, his tail straight up too, the smaller chunk of elk meat on the ground between them. Standing behind Raze, like bodyguards, were Lupa and Ben. Down the slope Hope was standing over Frick, clearly favoring her right leg as she ministered to his bloody wounds.

"Have some food, Blue Boy," Raze said. "It's elk, your favorite."

Blue Boy said nothing.

"Your ribs are showing," Raze said. "Those humans didn't feed you?"

"That's no concern of yours," Blue Boy snapped.

"Do something to your mouth, did you?"

"Time you shut yours."

"You don't look so good, old wolf. Did you wear yourself out?"

Blue Boy arched his neck, his fur standing on end, and let out a low snarl. "I'll wear you out."

But tossing the bigger chunk of meat into the den must have aggravated his poor gums, for the blood was now flowing freely from his mouth. Worse, he was wavering on his feet, as if standing in a high wind, when there wasn't so much as a breeze.

"Father!" Hope said in alarm.

As Raze crouched to attack, Lamar stepped out from behind the boulder. Hope twisted her head around. "Lamar!"

Everyone looked his way. Even Frick lifted his head off the ground and watched as Lamar climbed the hillside, weaving among tufts of new grass and splotches of melting snow. Raze rose out of his crouch and gave him a murderous glare. Blue Boy looked disgruntled.

"Taking a break from your coyote?" Blue Boy said.

As Lamar passed under my aspen, he shot me a look. Deservedly, as I had let the cat—or coyote—out of the bag. But he just kept climbing. He went right up between Blue Boy and Raze and ripped off about half of the remaining hunk of elk. After chewing a while, he crouched and swiveled toward Blue Boy, as if now *he* was going to challenge him. Every muscle in Blue Boy's shaky body stood out.

But all Lamar did was creep forward and give the bottom of Blue Boy's bloodied snout a kiss. Then he regurgitated the elk he'd just chewed onto the ground and moved off to Blue Boy's side. Lupa's eyes grew round as a deer's. Raze's blazed with fury. Lamar watched his father. Blue Boy sniffed, gave Lamar a dubious sidelong look, and sniffed again. He lowered his snout tentatively and sampled the pre-chewed elk.

It took him a little while, but Blue Boy devoured it all. The meal didn't staunch the flow of blood from his mouth, but it seemed to restore his stability. He swiped the grease and blood off his lips with his tongue and gave Lamar another sidelong glance before turning his gaze on his other son. Ben hung his head and stepped backward, his tail between his legs.

Then Blue Boy's eyes fixed on Raze. "What were you saying?"

If it had been anyone other than Raze, I would have pitied him. A moment ago he'd been about to dispatch the wobbly alpha and take over the pack. Now he was faced with two wolves, each bigger than he was—on the very spot where his father had humiliated him almost two years ago.

"Nothing," Raze muttered, his tail wilting.

21

SINCE STEPPING OUT FROM BEHIND THE BOULDER, Lamar had been the picture of calm, but now his eyes flashed and his ears bent forward, pointing directly at Raze.

"You did this to Frick?" he said.

Raze looked warily from Frick to Blue Boy to Lamar. I thought he was about to make some glib response when he spun around and flew off up the hill, spraying Lupa with mud. Lamar charged after him.

"Let him go," Frick rasped.

Lamar slid to a stop. Raze might not have been the biggest of wolves, but he was fast, and he was over the hill and out of sight in a flash. Lamar trotted back down the slope and joined his father and Hope at Frick's side. Ben was staring up the hill looking shell-shocked. Lupa must have been in shock too. She made no move to clean herself off, just stood there speckled with mud. Hope limped off into the woods and returned with some herbs from Frick's secret stash, which evidently wasn't secret to her.

While Hope tended to Frick, I told Blue Boy I'd been convinced he was dead when I left him in the compound. It turned out he'd come to, and Golden Hair had spent most of yesterday nursing him. She'd even poked him with a needle, as I'd seen Earflaps do with ailing horses.

"Then the other human came back in that noisy contraption," Blue Boy said.

"I hate to have to tell you this," I said, "but he'd been off hunting your brother."

"Uncle Sully?" Lamar said.

I nodded. "The human shot him."

"With the same kind of bullet they used on me?" Blue Boy asked.

"I'm afraid not," I said. "He's dead."

Blue Boy sucked in his breath and lowered his eyes to the soggy ground. Lamar looked stricken.

"Why would they do that?" Hope asked.

"He'd been killing cattle," I said.

"In Montana," Lamar said quietly.

"How do you know that?" Blue Boy said, turning to his firstborn son.

"I got to know him a little," Lamar said. "I liked him. Though I'm not sure he was always reliable." He glanced up at me. "There were no voles in the barranca."

"Sully was just trying to get you out of there," I said. "The human was coming with his rifle."

Lamar's eyes widened. So did Blue Boy's.

"You're sure he's dead, Maggie?" Blue Boy asked.

"I didn't leave him till the buzzards came."

"Poor Uncle Sully," said Hope.

For a while the only sound was the gurgling of the swollen creek. It made me think of Sully's fishing.

"He was quite a wolf, in his own way," I said. "I even saw him catch a fish."

"Really?" said Hope.

"He told me about the other owl," Lamar said quietly.

"What other owl?" Blue Boy said.

"The one who grabbed him when he was a pup."

"Oh, that."

"He told me other things too." Now it was Lamar's turn to study the ground. "I owe you an apology, Father."

After another silence Blue Boy said: "You just happened by today, did you?"

Lamar glanced up at me again.

"Ah, well, you don't owe me a thing," Blue Boy said gruffly.

Hope went back to licking the wounds on Frick's scarred backside. I asked Blue Boy if the humans had driven him back this way in their four-wheeler before releasing him.

"They didn't release me," he said.

"Then how'd you get here?"

"Last night they put me in one of their pens. Same one as years ago. They'd filled in the hole Sully and I dug, but they hadn't packed it very well. After I got through that, it was easy."

This explained the dirt all over him.

He must have been as tired as he was filthy, for while Hope fussed over Frick, Blue Boy's head began to nod, and he soon curled up by the den entrance and fell sound asleep. I caught a short nap myself. When I woke up, no one had moved much except Lupa, who was nowhere to be seen. I asked Lamar, who was lying under my tree, where she'd gone.

"She left," he said simply.

I was a little surprised that she would follow Raze after his ignominious retreat, especially considering he'd splattered her precious fur with mud. On the other hand, staying with the pack wouldn't have been an attractive option. Having chosen the wrong side, she would have been in deep disgrace, demoted to the bottom of the pecking order. Plus, she would soon have had to watch Alberta come parading out with her new litter. What surprised me more was that Ben was still here. By not going along with her, he was alone in his shame.

Just before nightfall Blue Boy roused himself and went to stand sentinel at the top of the hill. I couldn't imagine Raze and Lupa coming back to make a sneak attack, but when I flew up to the poplar sapling he informed me that humiliated wolves could be dangerous. Toward dawn he dozed off at his post, and not long afterward Lamar woke up and slipped away. I stayed put. I figured I knew where he was going.

The sky was still socked in, so there was no sunrise to speak of. But as the daylight brightened, Blue Boy woke up.

"Lamar went back to that fool coyote, I suppose?" he said, eyeing me.

Though Artemis had managed to get cornered by mountain lions, I didn't think of her as foolish, but I let it go. "I imagine so," I said.

"Well, I appreciate your going for him. Things might have gotten a little dicey otherwise."

For Blue Boy this was quite an admission.

As the other wolves stirred, we went down the hillside. An ugly new scab had formed on Frick's rear end, but when Blue Boy asked how he was feeling he said he was much better.

"I'll get us something to eat," Blue Boy said.

"No, you won't," said Frick.

"Excuse me?"

"Open your mouth."

"What did you say?"

"I said, 'Open your mouth.'"

If anyone else had given Blue Boy an order like that, I'm sure fur would have flown. But after a moment Blue Boy actually did open his mouth. Frick inspected his teeth and gums and announced that hunting was out of the question.

"If you go, you'll regret it the rest of your life. Which, by the way, will be very short."

Blue Boy snorted.

"You have to face facts, old boy," Frick said. "You've lost an incisor. You'll never be quite the same. But if you don't give the other teeth time to heal you'll lose them, too, and you'll be as useless as me."

"You're not a bit useless," Hope said.

"You're staying home, Blue Boy," Frick said firmly. "Besides, if you went, you might miss the pups."

This last argument may have tipped the scales, for after a long look at the den Blue Boy sank down on his haunches. Hope volunteered to go look for some food, but she'd clearly landed badly when Raze threw her, and Frick vetoed this, too. Blue Boy turned to Ben, who was sitting hunched like a whipped dog a short distance away.

I suppose it was a moment similar to when Blue Boy looked at Sully through the chain-link fence at the compound, expecting him to come through their tunnel. Like his uncle, Ben failed the test. He'd never been as bright or as brave as Lamar, and either he didn't realize he'd been given an opportunity to redeem himself or he was scared to go on the hunt by himself. He didn't move a muscle.

Then the moment was gone. I'd assumed Lamar had gone back to the knoll, but now he came trotting down off the ridge trail carrying an enormous hunk of elk in his mouth.

"Hope did all the work," he said after depositing the meat by the den. "There's still plenty left on that bull you brought down. Come with me, Ben."

Ben didn't need to be asked twice. He hopped to and followed Lamar onto the ridge trail. The pair of them carried back enough food to last everyone two or three days. The choicest piece went into the den. Lamar chewed up the next-best chunk for his father, and though Blue Boy wasn't happy about it, he ate the mushy meal.

The weather remained gray for the next couple of days. Alberta remained in the den with the pups. Frick's clawed backside began to give him less pain, and my reinjured wing was soon back to normal. Blue Boy's mouth and Hope's leg began to heal too, but on the morning the food ran out, Frick was adamant that they let Lamar and Ben do the hunting. I accompanied the two brothers. I knew how changeable the young can be—hadn't I myself switched allegiance from Dan to Trilby in the space of a minute?—and just as Ben had once idolized Raze, he now seemed to idolize Lamar and followed him like a shadow.

When we reached the promontory, we could see two big herds of elk, but no strays. Lamar picked out an independent-minded pronghorn and chased her into a sinkhole with Ben right on his heels. As the pronghorn tried to scramble up one of the muddy sides, the two young wolves pounced on her.

I had a bite of breakfast and settled on one of the pronghorn's horns as Lamar and Ben started ripping off a haunch to take back. As they were cutting through the last tendons, I let out a squawk. Raze and Lupa were looking down at us from the rim of the sinkhole, their ears pitched forward aggressively. Lamar backed away from the carcass, bristling.

But the two older wolves weren't focused on him. "Hey, Ben," Raze said. "You've got to see our new territory over by Trout Lake."

Ben looked up at his old hero.

"We've missed you, Ben," Lupa purred.

Even with his snout and whiskers dripping with blood, Ben looked callow and vulnerable. As his eyes shifted uncertainly between Lamar and the pair of wolves up above, I realized that if he turned on Lamar it would be three wolves against one. But this time Ben passed his test. He moved over to stand shoulder to shoulder with his brother. When Lamar snarled and squinted at the intruders, Ben mimicked him perfectly.

Raze and Lupa exchanged a look of surprise. Lamar

started scrabbling up the side of the sinkhole, with Ben on his heels. By the time they were up top, Raze was racing away with Lupa in his wake. Soon they were no more than a ripple in the tall grass.

The brothers slid back down into the sinkhole and returned to their task. I'd flown up to watch but now settled back on my perch.

"Well done, Ben," I said.

He gave me a bloody grin.

A whole haunch was an ambitious undertaking, and watching the two of them drag it out of the sinkhole was pretty comical: Lamar scrambling backward, pulling from the top, while Ben pushed from below. Lamar slipped back down several times before they finally got the haunch out, by which time it was caked with mud. Dragging it along through the grass cleaned it off some, but it got filthy again on the slog up the promontory.

On the ridge trail we had to make pit stops so Lamar and Ben could rest their jaw muscles. And there were other delays. Lamar may have been a full year old now, but his curiosity was undiminished. He had to pause on the side of the trail to examine a snakeskin, and a verbena with little starry flowers. He had to gawk at a streak of lightning brightening the gloom to the west. He even chased a small, furry animal with round ears across a stretch of frost-shattered stone, calling out to ask what it was. Of course the terrified creature dove into a crevice without answering. When Lamar got back to the trail, I told him I thought it was called a pika.

"They're so cute!" he cried. "I can't wait to tell . . ." His voice trailed off.

"Frick?" Ben guessed.

Lamar grunted and clamped his jaws around the haunch. I suspected he was trying hard to ban Artemis from his thoughts so he could do his duty by his father and the pack.

It was almost dark by the time they got their prize home. After sticking a choice chunk in the den entrance, Lamar chewed some up for his father. Blue Boy made a face when he sniffed his portion.

"Sorry, it's not elk," Lamar said.

"Pronghorn's splendid," Frick said. "Easier to digest."

Frick and Hope dug in, and so did Lamar and Ben. In time Blue Boy took a few grudging nibbles, muttering between bites that this would be his last meal of baby food. More jagged streaks of lightning tore the fabric of the sky, and as Blue Boy headed up the hill to stand sentinel, it started to rain. I flew up to the poplar sapling to keep him company. Tired as Lamar must have been from his hunting and hauling, he climbed up there too. Of course Ben followed him.

"I'm not sure you need to stand watch anymore, Father," Lamar said through the pattering drops. "We saw Raze and Lupa today."

"What happened?" Blue Boy said

"They ran like field mice," Ben said. "I can't believe I ever fell for them."

"Hmp," Blue Boy said. "Sounds like you deserve a good night's sleep, Ben."

Something in Blue Boy's tone told Ben to detach himself from his new hero and turn in. Once he was gone, Blue Boy cleared his throat.

"I think I can handle things now," he said.

"I never thought you couldn't," Lamar said.

"What I mean is, feel free to go back to that silly coyote of yours, if you've a mind to."

"She's not silly, Father."

Blue Boy sniffed. "Get some sleep, Lamar."

Lamar sighed and trudged back down the slope in the rain.

22

THE RAIN TURNED INTO A DOWNPOUR. Neither the poplar sapling nor my aspen were fully leafed out yet, so I took refuge in one of the lodgepole pines. I slept fitfully, for even there I got dripped on. But at some point after midnight the clouds finally pulled up stakes and cleared the field for a glittering army of stars.

We all woke to a glorious sunrise. As I flew back to my aspen, everything on the slope above Slough Creek seemed to be lit from within: blades of grass, dandelions, even rocks. So did Blue Boy. The rain had washed his coat clean, and as he descended the slope in the slanting sun, his bluish fur had a fine sheen to it. Then Blue Boy did something he hadn't done in a long time: gave the call of the hunt.

"For heaven's sake, Blue Boy," Frick said.

"We're all still stuffed, Father," Hope said.

"I'm in the mood for some elk," Blue Boy declared.

"But you were up all night," Ben said.

"Give your teeth another day off," Frick advised.

"My teeth are fine," Blue Boy said, lifting his head proudly. "If nobody wants to come with me, I'll go alone."

But before he could trot off, Hope squealed. A floppy-eared pup came bumbling and blinking out of the den. Four others quickly followed, not a runt among them. When Alberta appeared in their wake, she seemed to have an inner glow, too.

The pups wagged their tiny tails, yipping and sniffing one another's noses and ogling the blossoming world around them. But when Blue Boy knelt down they all fell silent and filed up in an orderly manner to do obeisance, touching the bottom of his snout with theirs. There were three females and two males.

"The firstborn?" he said, eyeing the biggest of them.

"Isn't she a beauty?" Alberta said.

The firstborn really was gorgeous—and she had a bluish tinge to her fur!

"She takes after you, Father," Hope said.

"What shall we call her?" Frick said.

"Bluebell?" Hope suggested.

"Sounds more like a flower than a wolf, doesn't it?" said Frick.

"Other ideas?" Blue Boy said.

He looked at Alberta, but it was Lamar who spoke.

"How about Maggie?" he said.

"Maggie," said Blue Boy. "You know, I like that."

As a rule I'm surefooted, but somehow I lost my grip on my branch and had to beat my wings like an idiot to keep from tumbling to the ground.

"Come here, Maggie," Alberta said.

The biggest pup galloped over to her and nuzzled her belly.

"What a bright little thing!" Hope gushed.

For the rest of the day I couldn't take my eyes off my namesake. Blue Boy couldn't tear himself away either, so in the end his teeth and gums did get another day of rest. All the pups were irresistible—and irrepressible. They frisked and cavorted, their tails wagging madly, their yips drowning out the best efforts of my feathered colleagues across the creek. Ben joined in their games as if he was still a pup himself. Lamar was a little more subdued, but the pups would have none of it. To entice him to play, they spanked the ground with their front feet, and if that didn't work, they nipped him. They never let up till dusk, when one by one they collapsed in furry little heaps. Young Maggie lasted the longest.

After Alberta carried the pups back into the den, Blue Boy, who hadn't slept the night before, conked out by the den entrance. Hope, her eyes on the den, let out a sigh.

"Oh, Frick," she said, "wouldn't it be nice if we . . ."

"What?" Frick said. Then he seemed to catch her drift. "I'm afraid only the alpha pair mates, my dear."

"But I heard you and Lupa had a litter," Hope said. "You weren't the alpha pair."

"That was an unusual situation."

Blue Boy half opened an eye. "You never know," he said drowsily, "when another unusual situation might crop up."

He dozed off again. When a happy Hope and Frick followed suit, Lamar got up to stand sentinel, but Ben beat him to it, hurtling up the slope. Ben stationed himself on the crest of the hill, his ears cocked for the slightest noise. But after the way he'd thrown himself into the pups' sport I doubted he would last long, and sure enough by moonrise he'd collapsed in a furry heap himself.

Lamar climbed to the hilltop, and I flew to my poplar

sapling. It was breezy up there, but the warmest night yet. Wolves were howling off to the east, where the moon looked like a big yellow wolf's eye on the horizon, and to the north as well, but I didn't pick up Raze's voice or Lupa's among them. Lamar turned his head regularly, listening to each quadrant, though he never looked directly to the southeast.

Still there was no missing Artemis's howl. She really was a musical creature. It was almost as if she had some bird in her. Lamar howled back. Wolf howls are haunting but rarely cheerful, yet this one was. Artemis replied, running a scale in a series of happy quavers. I'd never heard anything quite like it.

I must have been as enthralled as Lamar, for I didn't hear the approaching steps any more than he did.

"Unusual howl."

Lamar's head whipped around. Blue Boy stopped directly under my sapling.

"I thought you were dead to the world," Lamar said.

"Just checking on things."

Lamar hung his head. "I guess I'm not much of a sentinel."

"Better than some," Blue Boy said, shifting his eyes to Ben's sleeping form. "Anybody can get distracted."

Again Artemis's howl wafted through the night.

"Maybe I did hear it once," Blue Boy said thoughtfully. "A year ago—the night you poked out of the den when you were still just a fuzz ball. It's kind of nice."

"Nice?" Lamar cried, his head shooting up. "It's unique!" After a pause he added, "That means—"

"I know what it means," Blue Boy said. "An example would be my firstborn son, eh, Maggie?"

What could I do but agree?

"By the way, I hope you don't mind our naming that pup after you," Blue Boy went on, keeping his eyes on me. "We probably should have asked your permission."

There was a time when I wouldn't have thought much of having an earthbound creature like a wolf pup named after me. But as I looked at the two pairs of glittering yellow eyes below me I realized that, wise as he'd been, Jackson had been wrong about one thing: some wingless creatures did have souls.

Ben's legs started scissoring against the ground, as if he was chasing something in a dream. When he hadn't taken the cue to hunt for the pack a couple of days ago, I'd figured he was in the doghouse for good, but he'd gotten another chance today in the sinkhole and redeemed himself. Sully had gotten a second chance as well, though in his case it had come too late. As for me, I'd done a lousy job with my first family on the Triple Bar T, but maybe I'd gotten a second chance too.

"Are you sure you want to saddle that adorable pup with 'Maggie'?" I said. "It's such a dull name."

"I like it," Blue Boy said.

"I think it's beautiful," Lamar added.

I almost fell off my limb again.

"The way I see it, Maggie," Blue Boy said, "you saved me in Montana, and again in Idaho, and again here in Yellowstone. None of us would be here if it weren't for you."

Now I lost my voice along with my balance. It was as if my heart had swollen so much, it had blocked my windpipe.

"You're not annoyed to have the firstborn named for you, are you?" Lamar said, giving me a look of distress.

I had to swallow twice, but I finally managed to speak.

"No, Lamar, I'm not annoyed," I said. "Not annoyed at all."

FIRSTBORN

BY TOR SEIDLER

DISCUSSION TOPICS

1. Maggie's personality comes through immediately in the narrative. How does she change throughout the novel?

2. Jackson tells Maggie that "you can't be loyal to others if you're not loyal to your own nature first." What does it mean to be "loyal to your own nature"? Do you think Maggie succeeds in doing so?

3. According to Jackson, "Only winged creatures have souls." What do you think Jackson means by having a soul? Why does Maggie conclude that "some wingless creatures did have souls"?

4. What else does Maggie learn from Jackson? How does he know so much?

5. Names are important throughout the story. How does Maggie feel about her name, and why? What does it mean to her when Blue Boy names one of his children after Maggie?

6. Maggie and Blue Boy are firstborns, which is "a big deal to wolves." Which other characters are firstborn? Why is being a firstborn important to wolves? Why do you think the author chose *Firstborn* as the title?

7. How do Maggie and Blue Boy become friends? How is their relationship useful to each of them? Blue Boy admits that Maggie has saved his life more than once. How did Maggie save his life? When have the wolves saved Maggie's life?

8. Think about the appearances and personalities of Alberta, Frick, Lupa, and Raze. How do they interact with each other? How does the dynamic of the pack change at different points, and why?

9. After Maggie hurts her wing, she thinks she may never fly again. However, she eventually regains her ability to fly and

realizes that, "You have to lose something to appreciate its true value." What does she mean? Do you agree? Is this true for any experiences in your life, or anyone you know?

10. Lamar is different from the other wolves in several ways. Reflect on those differences and how they affect what happens to him. Why does Maggie feel a "real connection" with Lamar?

11. Discuss the relationship between Blue Boy and Lamar. How are they alike and how are they different? What do they agree about? What causes tension between them?

12. Blue Boy tells Lamar to "assert your dominance." What does Blue Boy mean? How does Lamar assert his dominance? What are the consequences?

13. Artemis asks Lamar if he's in a hierarchy. What is a hierarchy? Can you name the hierarchies among different wolves in the novel? Where does Blue Boy fit in the hierarchy of his wolf pack?

14. Life in the wild is dangerous. Identify some of the injuries that the wolves suffer, and discuss how they deal with them.

When Sully is hurt, Maggie observes, "hope is the best medicine in the world." What does she mean by that?

15. Discuss the relationship between Blue Boy and Sully, and why Blue Boy is angry with Sully. Compare their relationship to the one between Lamar and Ben, noting similarities and differences.

16. When Sully dies, Maggie says she knows "how littered life is with death." Talk about the deaths of some of the characters, including Jackson and Sully, and how they affect Maggie and others.

17. How important is the element of setting in this novel? Could it have taken place somewhere else? Why or why not? Consulting the maps, describe different places that Maggie lives and travels, and identify the ones you think are most important to her fate.